SHE SEEMED TO
BELONG HERE

She stared down at the diamond ring she had been holding so tightly when the rescue squad had found her. She warned herself not to panic, but still it came—the awful shaking that made her cling tightly to the tower wall.

"I'm Roslyn—Roslyn Brant," she whispered as terror swept over her.

"Good evening, Juliet," said a voice behind her.

Roslyn stood still like a hunted creature as Duane drew nearer. "Why did you call me—that?"

"I couldn't resist it," he drawled. "The balcony scene. Ah, but I'm forgetting…you've lost your memory."

"That was cruel, Mr. Hunter. I want to remember—to know what it felt like to have love, even if I now have lost it."

HARLEQUIN CELEBRATES

Thirty-five Years of Excellence

These books may be available at your local bookseller.

Don't miss any of our special offers. Write to us at the following address for information on our newest releases.

Harlequin Reader Service
P.O. Box 52040, Phoenix, AZ 85072-2040
Canadian address: P.O. Box 2800, Postal Station A,
5170 Yonge St., Willowdale, Ont.   M2N 6J3

Violet Winspear

Court of the Veils

Harlequin Books

TORONTO • NEW YORK • LONDON
AMSTERDAM • PARIS • SYDNEY • HAMBURG
STOCKHOLM • ATHENS • TOKYO • MILAN

Original hardcover edition published in 1968
by Mills & Boon Limited

ISBN 0-373-15103-9

Harlequin edition first published January 1969
Second printing July 1972
Third printing (as part of Harlequin Omnibus 6) September 1974

Harlequin Salutes edition published August 1981
Harlequin Celebrates Thirty-Five Years of Excellence
edition published November 1984

Printed in U.S.A.

CHAPTER ONE

THE plane crashed in the desert during a storm. There were not many survivors, but among them was the fiancée of Armand Gerard.

The young Frenchman had been travelling home to the date-palm plantation owned by his family at El Kadia in the Sahara. Roslyn Brant had been with him; a young airline hostess on leave whom Armand had been planning to introduce to his family after a whirlwind courtship.

Now Armand was dead, and Roslyn lay a victim of amnesia in a hospital run by the gentle-faced nuns of El Kadia, a desert oasis which had flourished over the years into a city of palms, arcaded streets, and villas above the Temcina Lake.

Most of Roslyn's clothing had been torn off in the crash, and though unconscious when taken to the hospital she held tightly in her right hand a lovely engagement ring set with a single blazing diamond. The ring she had doubtless been admiring just before the crash, studying, perhaps, the words carved inside the rose-gold band. 'We will always be together,' they said, so simply and trustfully.

Armand's family had been informed by letter that he was bringing his English fiancée to the plantation known as Dar al Amra, and a few weeks after the crash Armand's grandmother told Roslyn firmly that she was to come and recuperate at the plantation and try to find the peace of mind that might help her to regain her memory. It was perhaps a blessing in disguise, the Frenchwoman added, that at present Roslyn could remember nothing of the storm, the crash, and the tragic death of her fiancé.

Even her name had been a blank to her. Other people

had to tell her that she was a twenty-two-year-old airline hostess, whose home in England was a hostel near Airfield in Middlesex.

'My poor *petite*.' Madame Gerard patted Roslyn's hand. 'Tomorrow you will be out of this place. You will come home to us, and to have you there will be like having a small piece of Armand.'

'But I – I can't impose myself on you, *madame*.' Roslyn looked troubled and uncertain. 'You don't have to feel responsible for me just because—'

'Because Armand loved you and wished to marry you?' Madame Gerard looked affronted, icy in a moment as her snow-blue hair. 'We of Dar al Amra wish you to stay with us out of concern for your welfare, and the love you had for Armand. We are not offering you charity!'

Roslyn flushed sensitively. 'I'm sorry, *madame*, for being so stiff-necked,' she apologized. 'It's most kind and generous of you to want me to stay a while at the plantation.'

'You are *anglaise*,' Madame shrugged with Gallic eloquence. 'I had a son-in-law who could be, as you call it, stiff-necked in his British pride. All is forgiven *petite*, if I hear no more talk of you imposing yourself on us.' And Madame Gerard smiled, little eyelines showing through make-up applied so skilfully that her true age was difficult to assess. Her dress of grey silk had Paris written all over it, her hat was brimmed with shadow-lace that enhanced eyes still as blue as anchusas.

'Until tomorrow, my child.' She bent over Roslyn and kissed her cheek. '*Au revoir*.'

'*Au revoir, madame*.' And the scent of anchusas lingered in that hospital room after the indomitable *éminence grise* of Dar al Amra had made her departure.

Madame Gerard had loved her youngest grandson very much, Roslyn reflected, and for about the hundredth time she took into her hands the photograph of Armand

Gerard which she had asked for, and studied his lean handsome face, and smiling Gallic eyes under peaked eyebrows.

For a long while Roslyn sat holding the photograph, a quiet and tearless Cinderella whose glass slipper had smashed, whose Prince Charming was dead. Only the glitter of his ring proved that she had known and loved the young man who seemed a total stranger to her. She rose from the cane armchair in which she was resting and went across to a plain mirror that hung on the wall. She studied the rain-grey of her own eyes, the clipped fairness of her hair, the nose, mouth and chin that had nothing very dramatic about them. What had Armand seen in her? He was so handsome in his photograph that he would have been forgiven for loving a raving beauty rather than a boy-slim creature like herself – who might have looked a bit more striking before the disaster and the loss of shoulder-length hair. Most of it, Madame Gerard had told her, had been sheared off in the operating theatre.

Roslyn Brant. She spoke the name aloud. Her brows, several shades darker than her hair, puckered with the effort she made to remember. Roslyn – Armand . . .

They might have been names in a book for all the personal meaning they had for her. Her memory was gone, like smoke in her face, and all that was left was the sudden smart of tears. But for the kindness of the Gerard family she would be going back to England, which seemed far more distant and strange to her than this place called El Kadia.

Madame Gerard had talked a little about the plantation, which ran to many miles of the finest and most fertile date-palms in the Sahara and was under the supervision of her grandson, Duane Hunter. His father had been the proud and stiff-necked Britisher, as Madame had put it, who had married her daughter Céleste and taken her to live on a very different plantation out in

7

British Guiana. Céleste had died there when the boy was about ten years old. Duane had grown up in the bush, receiving his education in England and returning later to manage with his father a large Government-owned plantation.

Four years ago, when Duane was twenty-seven, his father had decided after almost a lifetime to go home to England. About the same time Madame Gerard had contacted Duane and asked him to come to Dar al Amra to run things for her. Her son who for many years had helped her to manage the place had died. Armand was still being educated in Europe, while Tristan, his brother, was more interested in the composition of music than the production of dates.

Roslyn, fascinated by the name of the plantation, Dar al Amra, had asked what the words meant. 'They mean House of the Master,' Madame had smiled. 'The plantation house was long ago the residence of a wealthy Aga who had a large harem, and our main patio is called the Court of the Veils.'

Despite the bleakness of having her entire past swept from her mind, Roslyn was looking forward to going to Dar al Amra to live for a while among these French plantocrats. Madame Gerard had been a famous stage actress before her marriage. Nina Nanette, the toast of Paris, she had told Roslyn, until Armand Gerard senior strode, desert-tanned, into her life, drunk champagne from her slipper and captivated her for always.

'Such men are not often made,' she had sighed. 'How they can love and wound, and make life a heaven and a hell! A woman might find peace with a gentler man, but how she would miss the fighting and the making up.'

'Was – the younger Armand like his grandfather?' Roslyn had asked.

'Your Armand was charming, gay-hearted, a nice boy,' Madame told her. 'He would have made life very pleasant

8

for you – but we must not talk about that. You have enough to bear, the injury to your poor head and the losing of your memory.'

It felt strange, frightening not to know anything about herself beyond what other people told her. She had no family in England, and only very recently had she learned that her best friend, a girl without family like herself, had been one of the air hostesses who had died when the plane had crashed.

Her name had been Juliet Grey and she had lived at the same hostel as Roslyn.

Roslyn's remaining hours as a patient passed swiftly, and true to her promise Madame Gerard arrived early the next morning to take Roslyn home with her. Very little passenger luggage had been salvaged from the crash, and Nanette – as Madame insisted upon being called – had gone shopping the day before and bought Roslyn a set of lingerie to go under a cool linen dress; a smart pair of sandals, a handbag in raffia and a shady hat to match.

Roslyn just didn't know how to thank her. Nanette waved away her thanks with a tiny hand, more concerned with the fit of the dress and highly pleased that the white tube was just right on Roslyn's boy-slim figure. There was a lipstick and a compact of cream-powder in the handbag and she watched critically as Roslyn applied them. 'Don't be shy with the lip colouring, my child,' she exclaimed. 'Your pale features need emphasis – ah, but wait until you have lived in the desert sun for a while! The sun will turn you into a real blonde – I wonder if you can ride? *En tout cas*, Tristan or Duane will teach you. There is nothing better for the circulation than an early morning gallop on a good horse.'

Roslyn caught her breath at the idea, quite certain somehow that she had never been on a horse in her life.

'I wouldn't mind learning how to ride,' she smiled.

'Aren't Arab horses rather fierce?'

'Of course,' Nanette said imperturbably. 'But you are not a timid child. How could you be when you worked as an air hostess, and loved a Gerard?'

'Are the Gerards so intimidating?' Behind Roslyn's smile there lurked a sudden strange fear – a fear she couldn't account for in view of the kindness Madame Gerard had so far shown her.

'We live on the edge of the desert, so perhaps it has made us a little savage in some respects.' Madame shrugged and pulled on her gloves. 'Now we depart, my child, for Dar al Amra. Are you excited?'

Roslyn nodded, and as they walked out of the hospital she smiled goodbye at the kindly nuns and felt apprehensive of her meeting with Duane Hunter, and Tristan. Madame had said that Tristan was working on an opera based on an old legend about the favourite of the Aga of Dar al Amra. Her name had been Nakhla, grace of the palm, and a French officer had fallen in love with her. Assuming the guise of a veiled visitor, he had manged more than once to get into the harem to see Nakhla. The Aga found them out, and had the handsome head of the Frenchman presented to his favourite in a jewel casket!

Roslyn had an idea she was going to have tastes in common with Tristan, but his cousin sounded tougher, more formidable.

A car with a uniformed Arab driver waited at the gates of the hospital, and soon they were honking their way through the busy city streets, where tiers of flat-roofed houses caught the sun on their walls of limewash, ochre and cobalt blue. Arcaded lanes were honeycombed with Eastern shops, above which the strange Hand of Fatma was carved or pressed into the plaster.

Through the open windows of the car there came a spicy-plummy-goaty smell, and Roslyn leaned forward eagerly to take in the passing Arabs of all shades, a mosque of white stucco, blue-domed, with a lace-like minaret, and the camels that hung lugubrious heads over the gate of a *fondouk*.

'It's like being in another world,' she breathed. Her eyes met those of the woman beside her, whose expression was thoughtful and sad, as though she had Armand on her mind and the boyish pleasure he would have got out of showing the attractions of El Kadia to his English bride-to-be.

Soon the city was left behind and they were speeding along a road cut through the desert. It was now mid-morning and the sun was burning overhead, the cause of crests and troughs in the road which their driver had to take at high speed in order to save his passengers from too much bumping. Though the big car was air-conditioned, Roslyn was beginning to feel the heat. The crests of sand dazzled her eyes, a vibrating landscape with serrated hills in the distance, like stairs leading into the sky.

'That is the Gebel d'Oro,' Nanette told her. 'Seen close to, those hills are a strange colour, like petrified flames – Barbary bandits are said to have a stronghold there.'

'In this day and age?' Roslyn exclaimed.

'This is the East, *chérie*.' Nanette fitted a cigarette into a holder and flicked her lighter at the tip. The smoke of a Caporal Jaune was sweet and strong in the car. 'Men of the desert will never be completely tamed, and that is one of its primitive pleasures, that the desert harbours wolves, leopards and hawks that are not always four-footed and winged.'

Roslyn studied her benefactress. 'The actress in you is still very fond of the dramatic situation, isn't it, Madame Gerard?' she said. 'Confess that I intrigue you because I have no memory? I am stormdrift, to whom you are offering your home like a castle of refuge.'

Nanette gave a soft little laugh. 'Yes, you intrigue me,

my child. I will admit that when I first saw you, bandaged, bruised, thin as a boy, I could not fathom your attraction for my handsome Armand. I can only suppose that he was beguiled by your air of retreat; your grey eyes that are clear as rainpools, and yet full of concealment.'

There was a brief, electrical silence. Roslyn could feel her heart pounding from the heat, and from what Nanette had said. Was there in the Frenchwoman's manner the hint of a question? Did she think that Roslyn had something to conceal . . . and that she concealed it behind the mask of a false amnesia?

She pulled her gaze from the blink of a large ruby on Nanette's hand, turned her head to the window to hide the little leap of pain in her eyes. The dense green of many palm trees lay to the left and right of them, towering, meeting overhead as they drove through the endless forest of Dar al Amra date-palms, along a smoothly cleared track that was shaded from the burning sun by the huge palmate leaves of the giant trees.

Under the fingers of her right hand Roslyn could feel the carbuncle of a diamond set in the rose-gold band of Armand Gerard's ring. 'We will always be together,' he had said. But Roslyn could not remember him, or the moment when he had said those words and slipped the lovely ring on to her finger.

She could not remember – and she caught her breath as the song of a forest bird echoed through the trees, and the chirring of katydids filled the air. It was cool under the trees, green as a sea-cave, the track ahead spattered with arrowheads of gold that shot down through chinks in the canopy of leaves.

Roslyn glimpsed the white gowns of men working among the trees, and Nanette told her that soon they would harvest the fruit, grade it and pack it, and then transport it to the dock where it would travel by ship to many ports all over the world. The Dar al Amra dates were famous, Nanette added proudly. 'We have, also, almond trees, oranges and olives, apricots, quince and figs. Our soil is very fertile, fed from underground streams, you understand. Then again my grandson Duane is a man of ideas with the ability to carry them through, and the plantation is now producing many more side fruits than before he came here to supervise things for me.'

Great bunches of ripening amber fruit gleamed among the green, and when the car branched to the left, Nanette pointed out another section of the plantation where a white Moorish house stood alone, its walls ablaze under a cloak of bougainvillea red as dragon's blood. 'Duane wished to live alone when he came here,' his grandmother said, 'so he occupies the supervisor's residence. The house always seems very solitary to me, set among the trees, but Duane was determined.' Nanette laughed and stubbed her cigarette. 'He has a will of iron which bruises a woman until she gives in to him.'

Soon the solitary house of Duane Hunter was left behind, and they drove past row upon row of low, globular orange trees whose bouquet filled the air like a thousand and one weddings all taking place at the same time. Roslyn took deep breaths of it, and she was sure that all her life this moment would return to haunt her, when the Moorish entrance of Dar al Amra came into view, flanked by high tawny walls.

They drove under the great horseshoe into the Court of the Veils, where once upon a time the favourites of the harem had sauntered, their anklets tinkling at every step, their eyes demure or Persian-cat above gauzy yashmaks.

Roslyn climbed out of the car in something of a daze, and stood looking about her at the mosaic of tiling, the triangle of fountains and the great shade tree that gushed cascades of cool green all over the courtyard . . . there was something symbolic and enchanted about the tree. Its wonderful sprays of leaves might have been carved from jade.

'I don't think I could ever have seen anything more beautiful,' she said to Nanette, and as she turned to look at the older woman her grey eyes caught the sun and seemed alight.

'I prophesy that El Kadia has many more surprises in store for you,' Nanette smiled. 'Now let us go in – ah, do you hear music? That is my Tristan, playing part of the opera he is composing.'

They followed the piano music along a corridor of carved archways and it stopped as Nanette's high heels tapped across the tiled floor of the *salon,* a high cool room with a cedarwood ceiling, low divans and tables, glimmering oriental rugs and hammered lamps slotted with jewel-toned glass.

'*Grand'mère*!' The slender young man jumped to his feet and came over to them. He was in his early thirties, Roslyn guessed. Of middle height, with black hair threaded with grey, Latin eyes and the features of his dead brother!

Roslyn must have gone white, for even as Tristan bowed over her hand with a welcoming smile, his eyes were concerned, his fingers pressing warm about hers. '*Bienvenue,* Roslyn' he said. 'You are now feeling quite well?'

Like his grandmother he spoke excellent English, and Roslyn breathed a little sigh of relief. If she had in the past spoken a little French, it was now lost to her. Lost like everything that had happened before the crash. Lost like Armand . . . the lover who might have had a voice like Tristan's, and a touch that was warm and sympathetic.

'My mind is still a blank,' she said to him. 'But apart from that I feel quite fit, thank you, *m'sieur.*'

'You must feel like a newborn infant.' His smile showed a neat line of white teeth. 'I think myself that it would be

14

interesting to be reborn, fully adult and open to a brand new set of impressions and sensations.'

'You, my handsome satyr,' said his grandmother, 'will proceed to have coffee brought in for this child and myself. I am parched after that long drive, and Roslyn has already soaked up more than enough impressions for one morning.'

Tristan quirked an eyebrow at his elegant and lovely grandmother then he strolled to the central archway of the room and clapped his hands. A shape in white materialized, then vanished and Nanette sank with a sigh among the cushions of a divan.

'Sit down, child,' she ordered, and Roslyn perched herself on a tapestried hassock and again took shy stock of the room, the man and the black grand piano he had been playing. He lounged against it, regarding her without shyness and wearing a sand-coloured shirt outside black needlecord slacks. Roslyn's gaze fell suddenly away from his dark Latin one to the soft Arab slippers on his feet.

'What do you think of our desert domain?' he asked. 'Of being here in the land of the fatalists?'

'I feel as though I have come from nowhere to a place I—' and there Roslyn hesitated, for what she felt could only sound melodramatic put into words.

'Do go on,' Tristan murmured, a trifle wickedly. 'I cannot bear to be left in suspense.'

'Well,' Roslyn saw the hint of wickedness in Tristan's smile, but it encouraged her rather than put her off, 'the strangeness of the desert doesn't unnerve me. It's as though I was meant to come here.'

'A very natural feeling in the circumstances,' Nanette put in dryly. 'Armand was bringing you here, was he not? He must have talked to you about his desert family and though you cannot remember the things he said, you accept us because of them.'

'What a very practical mind you have for a lovely

woman, Nanette,' Tristan mocked affectionately.

Nanette smiled at her pearl-varnished fingernails and looked the coquette she must once have been. 'It is the gift of the Frenchwoman, *mon chéri*,' she said, 'to be able to be practical without any loss of charm.'

A silent-footed servant entered the room at that point, carrying a tray on which stood a steaming earthenware jug, large French coffee cups, and a plate of tasty-looking fruit tarts. The appetizing smell of freshly made coffee filled the room as Nanette poured out, and the trio were enjoying their coffee and cakes when sudden firm footfalls rang on the tiles beyond the central archway.

Roslyn on her hassock glanced up and saw framed in the Moorish archway a man in a bush hat that was bent down at one side. He removed the hat lazily, and a shaft of sunlight fired the dark bronze of his hair.

En garde! leapt into Roslyn's mind. There was so keen a quality about the man's tawny-green gaze that she felt a wild urge to shield herself from it. He was brown as rawhide from the desert sun, lean and hard and uncompromising as a lash that always found its mark.

'You are just in time for coffee, *mon brave*,' Nanette said to him. She glanced at Roslyn as she lifted the earthenware jug. A smile lit her blue eyes. 'Please not to look so apprehensive, child. This desert barbarian is my grandson Duane. Duane, meet the *petite fille* who was to have married our Armand.'

He crossed the room with long strides and stood over her. She had to tilt her fair head to look at him, a towering, booted challenge of a man.

'H – how do you do, Mr. Hunter?' She held out a hand, but he didn't take it. Thumbs in the slant pockets of his breeches, he stood quizzing her through the narrowed lids of a perpetual sun-dweller.

'So you are Roslyn Brant?' His voice matched his hard,

16

brown looks. 'Somehow I pictured you differently. Funny, eh?'

His tone was like the jib of a spur and Roslyn leapt recklessly to answer him. 'I pictured you exactly as you are, Mr. Hunter,' she said, 'and that isn't funny.'

CHAPTER TWO

'*Touché!*' Tristan was chuckling as his cousin sat down beside their grandmother and took the cup of coffee she had poured out for him.

'By the way, where is Isabela?' Tristan added. 'I understood that she was going to ride with you on your round of inspection.'

Duane emptied his cup of black coffee and held it out for more. 'Your operatic guest should stick to her singing,' he drawled. '*Merci*, Nanette, I'm dry as sand.'

'Don't tell me Isabela fell off her horse and you left her where she fell?' Tristan was looking amused as he fired a cheroot.

'Not quite.' Duane stretched his long, booted legs across an oriental carpet and disposed of a fruit tart in two hungry bites. 'I couldn't take all day playing the leisurely planter, so she had to keep up with me, more or less. When we got back ten minutes ago, she called me an unfeeling brute in her charming Portuguese, then hobbled off to her room to wallow in a cologne bath. No doubt she will soon make an entrance in a delectable concoction called a dress.'

'The girl is right, you are a brute, Duane.' His grandmother laughed, but Roslyn caught the note of nostalgia in her voice. 'If there is any *tendresse* in you, I swear you give it all to those ranks of date-palms with their crests in heaven and their roots in hell. Am I right, *mon brave*?'

'Are you ever wrong?' he drawled. And then very deliberately he glanced at Roslyn, not a smidgen of sympathy in his eyes only a glint that planted a swift dart of antagonism in her heart. Tristan was charming, but his cousin seemed to have little time or sympathy to spare for females . . . least of all for a piece of stormdrift like herself. When his glance dropped to the ring flaming on her left hand, the fingers of her right hand covered the diamond almost before she realized what she was doing. Her unguarded action at once brought a steely glint to his eyes, intensifying his look of a hunting hawk about to pounce on its prey . . .

Roslyn didn't realize that she was holding her breath until a woman's voice floated across the *salon* and broke the tension. She turned her head and saw dark eyes sparkling above a lace fan, held so that it concealed the lower part of the newcomer's face like a yashmak. The carved woodwork of the central archway was a perfect frame for her lovely figure, draped in a dress of silk the colour of sunlight.

'What did I say about that entrance?' Duane's laughter was indulgently mocking as he climbed to his feet, his tawny-green eyes upon Isabela Fernao as she lowered the fan to reveal her vivid Latin face.

'*Madre de Deos!*' She swept across to him and struck him none too lightly across his brown cheek with her folded fan. 'Never again will I rise early from my bed to ride with you, you tyrant of a man.'

'I didn't ask you to ride with me.' He grinned down at her, and though she was quite tall he made her look fragile. 'It was your idea to come and keep me company Doña Sol.'

'My name is Isabela.' Her eyes flashed their seductive danger straight into his.

'Doña Sol is the impression I get.' His glance swept her figure in the golden dress, and self-assured as she was she must have felt a twinge of shyness, for she turned from him fluttering her fan and laughing breathlessly behind its shield. Dark glossy hair framed her large Latin eyes.

Roslyn's eyes of rain-grey, under a boyish cap of fair hair, met and were held by those of Isabela Fernao. 'Ah,

19

you must be the affianced of poor Armand?' she exclaimed. 'The little English girl who was hurt in the head. How do you find yourself now, my dear?'

Was the query meant to be kind, or did it hold a hint of condescension? Isabela's brown eyes were flecked with gold, and pointed were the long fingernails that played with the fan she used so alluringly. Her body had a seductive grace which made Roslyn seem almost childish – even elfish – perched as she was on a hassock.

'I find myself in a very interesting household, *senhorita*,' Roslyn replied, with a tilt to her pointed chin.

'Ah, the pixie out of an English dell speaks up for herself.' Isabela sank down among the cushions of a divan and purred a laugh as she took stock of the ensemble which Madame Gerard had bought for Roslyn. The plain white dress emphasized her youthfulness, and her sandals revealed unvarnished toes which curled together as Latin eyes appraised her.

'What will you have to drink, Isabela?' Nanette was regarding the lovely Latin with amused eyes. 'The coffee is still hot, or there is fruit cup.'

'I would love a glass of *heloua*.' Isabela shared a drowsy smile between the two men; it was Tristan who went to the table on which stood a pitcher of orange-juice with an ice-filled cylinder inside to cool the juice. He poured Isabela a glass and brought it to her. 'Will you have a cake with it?' he asked.

'A *flan de cerises, mon ami*.' Her lips were as cherry-ripe as the fruit in the flan, and she obviously revelled in male attention.

'It must be very strange for you, not to have any recollection of yourself,' she said to Roslyn. 'Have you forgotten *everything*?'

Roslyn, conscious of steel-green eyes through cheroot smoke, tightened her arms about her knees. 'I can remember nothing that is personal to me,' she said quietly. 'The faces of people and the places I knew are like dreams I can't recall. They elude me like ghosts. I – I grope after them, but they just won't materialize.'

'And will it always be like that for you?' Like many people with artistic talent, Isabela was completely self-absorbed; the look in her eyes was one of avid curiosity rather than sympathy.

Roslyn saw this and she gave a cold little shiver at the detachment of other people from one's fears and heart-aches. Nanette was kind, but even she had looked at Roslyn with tiny clouds of doubt in her eyes. Tristan was charming because that was his way, but with a look that was explicit without words, Duane Hunter had intimated that his cousin Armand could never have loved and wanted a girl like herself. His tawny-green eyes had flicked from her hair to her thin, sensitive face, down the slim arrow of a body that would feel lost in a man's arms. 'Somehow I pictured you differently,' he had drawled.

'Now you know what the doctor said.' Nanette was regarding Roslyn with a frown between her delicately made-up eyebrows. 'Forget that you have forgotten and let your memory reawaken when it will. It is not to be forced. It awaits the key that will unlock the spell.'

'Like the Sleeping Beauty,' drawled Duane Hunter.

Isabela gave a giggle, as though Roslyn in the role of Sleeping Beauty was quite a joke. Her eyes met his, her glance appraised him, taking in the defiant virility of his brown throat, the shoulders that stretched free as the desert under the thin white shirt, the lean, whipcord length of him from his hips down to his dusty riding boots.

He mashed out his cheroot in a tray and straightened up. 'Well, I have some more work to do,' he announced, strolling towards the archway that led out of the room. 'Au 'voir.'

'Duane,' his grandmother's voice made him pause and glance back into the room, his bush hat already at a rakish angle over his eyes, 'do you really have to act all the time like a galley-slave tied to his oar?' she demanded.

His mouth pulled to one side in a sardonic smile. 'Don't you like the look of the accounts lately, *chère madame*?' he asked. 'I thought they were looking very robust.'

'Will the same be said for you if you impair your *vitalité*?' Nanette tapped a slender French heel against the carpet in her annoyance with him. 'You do not take enough *repos*. Like a hungry wolf you are always on the prowl.'

'*Chère madame, que j'adore.*' He grinned wickedly and gave his grandmother a bow. Then he was gone, his footfalls ringing on the tiles of the Court of the Veils. Nanette sat looking exasperated for a minute or so, then she got to her feet and informed Roslyn that she would show her to the room that had been prepared for her.

'What are you and I going to do, Tristan?' Isabela was a tawny curve on her divan, a creamy arm resting upon the cushions.

'We also are going to work, my diva.' He strolled to his piano. 'The *cri de coeur* of my operatic heroine is now ready and I wish to try out the song with you.'

Isabela sat up, her veil of langour suddenly discarded to reveal the musical artiste who loved to sing. 'You have completed Nakhla's song of the hairline between hating and loving?' she breathed. 'Ah, you worked on it while I was out riding with Duane!'

Tristan was busy turning over sheets of music. 'Nakhla is like a gauzy moth who dreads flame, yet she cannot resist the pain to which she submits herself,' he said thoughtfully. 'That is how I see her, Isabela. How I wish you to interpret her for me.'

'Your opera sounds like being an interesting one, Tristan.' His grandmother closed a hand about Roslyn's wrist.

'To love is to be burned in the flames of passion and disillusion, *grand'mère*.' He seated himself at the piano and shot her a smile.

'Your cynicism almost matches Duane's,' Nanette said tartly. 'Love can be a most enjoyable emotion, but you young people of today seem to regard it as a battle. I suppose we can all expect the finale of your opera to be a tragic one, *chéri*, though in all likelihood Nakhla was merely fascinated by her soldier admirer, and in love with her master. A woman cannot help loving her master.'

'You are an incurable romantic, *grand'mère*,' Tristan chuckled, and played a snatch from The Merry Widow. 'But how can I deny Isabela a swan-song when she *succumbs* so beautifully on stage?'

'*Donnez-moi, maestro*.' Isabela was at the piano demanding her music as Roslyn followed Nanette out of the *salon*.

The older woman gave Roslyn a side-glance of inquiry. 'My grandsons are very dissimilar in appearance, do you not think?'

'Tristan has the look of Armand,' Roslyn replied quietly.

Nanette drew in her breath. 'You are recalling him?' she asked.

'I only wish – no, *madame*, I'm judging from the photograph you let me have of Armand.' Roslyn glanced at his ring, the token of a love she tried in vain to remember. 'I can hear the *senhorita* singing. She has a lovely voice.'

'Life is most interesting for people who find a true vocation, that is why I have never discouraged Tristan in his pursuit after musical expression.' Madame gave a tiny shrug and tucked a hand through Roslyn's arm as they mounted a wrought-iron stairway to the second gallery of the house. 'There are the demands of the plantation, of course, but I have Duane and he is fully capable of handling the various sides of the business. He was trained in such supervision by his father, a stern but very able man, and as I grow older I lose my interest in business, squabbles among the workers, one thing and another. You understand?'

Roslyn gave her hostess a smile and thought her a wonder for her age. 'I am sure you have earned the leisure which you now have, *madame*,' she said.

'You must call me Nanette, child. I like to hear my old theatrical name on people's lips, for it is good to be able to recall the past – ah, forgive me, child! The trouble is that one can never feel the troubles and fears of another, unless that other is a much-loved husband or wife. Perhaps, who can tell, you will feel a sense of communication with Armand here in his home, eh? For here he was born. Here he grew into a youth. The house is permeated with his laughter, his gaiety and love of life—'

Nanette broke off with a sigh, withdrew her hand from Roslyn's arm and opened an oval-shaped, vermilion-coloured door set in the corridor along which they had been walking.

Roslyn's room at Dar al Amra was white-walled, and beamed with cedar. The bed was low, with tall posts holding back yards of misty net as a safeguard against the intrusion of insects. Squares of oriental carpet covered the floor, and the windows were narrow harem-lattices covered with *mesharabeyeh*. There were deep window recesses beneath the lattices filled with cushions, a carved cupboard for her clothes, and a carved chest with mirror-stand upon it, and powder bowls on little embroidered mats.

Roslyn absorbed the strange Eastern charm of the room, with its vermilion door and lattices contrasting with the whitewashed walls and dark-wood ceiling. She saw that sprays of pale oleander had been arranged in a copper pot on a low, palmwood table.

'You think you will like sleeping here?' Nanette inquired.

'I love the room already,' Roslyn assured her.

'Here long ago a favourite of the harem was probably kept,' Nanette pointed to the narrow windows, the deep recesses where the girl would have knelt to watch her lord and master down in the courtyard. 'The days of female seclusion in the East, when the master of the house handed to his fancy of the moment a coloured veil to indicate that she was to be brought to him that night.'

'What a catastrophe if the master wasn't attractive.' Roslyn knelt in one of the recesses and peered through the mesh of finely carved wood over the window. 'I wonder if any of the girls ever refused the dubious honour of the harem veil?'

'I doubt it, *chérie*,' Nanette chuckled. 'The Aga was said to be a fiercely handsome man, so there is every likelihood that the inmates of his harem fought to win a veil from him. These veils were added to their everyday wear. A particular favourite would probably be clad in little else.'

Roslyn turned to regard Nanette with lit-up eyes. 'I can understand why Tristan wishes to write an opera about Dar al Amra,' she said. 'There is a sort of magic in the air. A sense of the old intrigues plotted under the boughs of that wonderful old tree down in the courtyard.'

Nanette studied Roslyn, kneeling there on a heap of cushions, a finger of desert sunshine stroking her hair and the thin line of her cheek. 'You have a lot of imagination, haven't you, my child?' She spoke in a thoughtful tone of voice.

'I think I must have,' Roslyn agreed.

'Armand had very little,' Nanette said, and then she walked quickly across the room to the carved *armoire* and jerked open the door. About half a dozen youthful dresses hung inside, also some jaunty blouses and several pairs of bright, narrow trousers. Nanette's hand delved into the back of the cupboard and hangers rattled as she brought into view a fold or two of something white. 'These are your trousseau, sent to us from a London shop while you were in hospital.' Armand's grandmother turned to give Roslyn a long, considering look. 'My grandson must have intended his marriage to you to take place in El Kadia.'

Roslyn stared at the white lace dress now fully revealed in Nanette's hands.

'Along with the dress came a tiny cap of pearls, and slippers also of white – Duane was of the opinion that you should be shown these things as soon as possible.'

Roslyn slipped to her feet and approached to touch the dress. Something seemed to stir into life in her mind . . . she sensed, though could not say for certain, that once before she had touched this lacy, knee-length dress with its simple heart-shaped bodice.

Nanette showed her the Juliet cap and the slippers. Roslyn knew them with her fingertips!

'I – I had dresses,' she said, in a shaken voice. 'You need not have bought me one.'

'You lost weight in hospital, child.' Nanette returned the lace wedding dress to the back of the *armoire,* along with the cap and the slippers. She fingered the day dresses and those for evening wear. 'These will have to be slightly altered, I should think, to fit your present measurements. I have a sewing-machine. My maid, who is very adept with her fingers, will see to the alterations.'

'Thank you, *madame.*'

'Nanette!' Suddenly the tiny ringed hands of Madame Gerard were pressed one each side of Roslyn's face. Her fingers traced the thrust of the fey cheekbones and the hollows beneath them. 'We must build you up, Roslyn. You are thin like a crane, with eyes that swallow your face. Does it hurt that I showed you the dress in which you would have been married?'

'Seeing it must hurt you as well, Nanette.'

'Just so, it hurts. But Duane was right. He said that there is nothing else at Dar al Amra to remind you of the past. The white dress and the little cap of pearls *were* familiar to you. They jolted your mind, eh?'

Roslyn nodded. 'I know, though I can't remember, that I tried on the cap. I – think Juliet Grey must have been with me. I think we might have joked about the Juliet cap.'

'The poor little Juliet who was killed,' Nanette said sombrely. '*In sha Allah.* You will hear the Arabs say that very often, my child. If a thing must be, it will be. And now I will leave you to take a little rest. Beside your bed you will find a service bell. If you require anything, ring it and one of the servants will soon come. Jakoub speaks half a dozen languages, so you will have no trouble communicating with him.'

The vermilion door closed behind Nanette, and for a long moment Roslyn stood where she was, facing the mirrored door of the *armoire*. It gave back her reflection in a strange, shadowed way. Her face looked masked . . . that of a masquerader who had wandered into a house of strangers who were as uncertain of her as she was of them.

She went closer to the mirror and stared at her unfamiliar self. Her grey eyes still held some of the shock of that morning in hospital when she had first realized that she could not remember who she was. In tears and panic she had listened to the doctor telling her gently that the affliction was only the temporary result of her head injury, and that normal functioning of her memory would return – in time.

But it felt so awful not to be able to remember anything but nightmare fragments of the crash itself . . . the flare of fire, the sound of rending metal and screams. Her escape, they said, had been miraculous, and in time the pain and emptiness of losing her fiancé would grow more bearable.

Armand . . . she spoke the name aloud and tried desperately to remember the man for whom she would have worn the white lace dress, and the Juliet cap studded with tiny beads. Surely when you fell in love the heart and the senses were far more involved than the mind, yet here she stood with her heart as empty as her mind!

A shiver of self-doubt ran through her. Perhaps she had not loved Armand, but had agreed to marry him because he was a Gerard and could give her a fairly easy life. That could be the explanation, much as it repelled her . . . and something of the sort might have been in Duane Hunter's mind when he had stared at the ring on her finger.

With a sigh she started to explore her room and the adjacent alcove which had been converted into a bathroom. The water used at Dar al Amra was evidently tapped from the underground springs that fed its acres of date and fruit trees, and when Roslyn discovered a robe, bath-towels, soap and crystals, she ran a tub of lukewarm water and eagerly undressed to take a cool bath after that desert drive from the hospital.

Afterwards she felt relaxed, and in the long robe she curled among the cushions of a window recess and flipped through some French magazines on a palmwood table beside her. In a while there was a knock on the door and she called, 'Entrez!'

A robed servant came in carrying a tray; a dignified, smiling Arab who informed her in throaty English that he was called Jakoub and that at the orders of Madame he had brought luncheon to the young sitt in her room.

He arranged the various dishes on the palmwood table in front of her, shooting interested glances at her, and all the while informing her that her menu consisted of onion soup, little lamb cutlets with vegetables, and pancakes

28

with honey. 'Everything looks very tasty,' she assured him, with sudden appetite. 'Is Madame Gerard having lunch in her room?'

'Always Madame eats in her room at this time of day,' he replied, smiling and nodding approval as Roslyn broke a *brioche* and started on her soup. 'The sun at noon is like fire in the sky, and we at Dar al Amra do our utmost to conserve the health of our Lella.'

Roslyn glanced up at Jakoub, who had a superbly trimmed beard and who wore the pale green turban of a Mecca pilgrim. 'Madame informed me that you speak several languages,' she said admiringly. 'Your English is extremely good, Jakoub.'

'The *sitt* is more than kind to say so.' He gave her a grave bow. 'I travelled much in my youth with a great writer from your land, Mees Brant. He wrote many books about the East, and I should be gratified if you would like to read some of them.'

'I'd love to, Jakoub!' She was delighted. There had been books at the hospital, but all of them written in French, and her craving for a good read told her that she must be a bookworm.

Jakoub was only too happy to sort out for her a selection of the books written by the novelist he had once served. With pride he pointed out a couple of dedications to himself, and Roslyn – whose genuine interest in the books had won her a friend in this desert house – settled down after her lunch to enjoy a long, luxurious read.

Then around three o'clock there came an interruption in the shape of Madame's maid. She couldn't speak English, but managed to convey to Roslyn that she would alter a dress for her to wear that evening at family dinner downstairs. Roslyn – heart hammering as she touched the trousseau dresses – selected a pleated chiffon in misty blue-grey. She had to try it on, of course, and Maryam indicated that it needed taking in at the waist and hips.

She carried the dress away with her, and after she had gone Roslyn found herself restless, unable to settle down again with the book she had been enjoying.

She knelt in the recess, gazing down through the mesh-lattice at the Court of Veils. The great shade tree was quite still in the afternoon heat, and only the tinkling of fountain water and the chirr of katydids could be heard. The spicy scents of the plantation stole through the windows, that were without glass, and Roslyn found her thoughts wandering down the groves of palm trees to the Moorish house hidden away among them.

Duane Hunter's solitary house, where he lived surrounded by the tall trees to whom he gave most of his devotion.

Roslyn's first encounter with him came back vividly into her mind, the way he had stood looking at her from the carved entrance of the *salon*, the sun on the dark fire of his hair, tousled above eyes the colour of lichen on a craggy wall. The instant their eyes had met, Roslyn had felt him to be hostile and unwelcoming, and it was a relief to know that he lived apart in his own establishment.

Perhaps living for years in the jungle had hardened him, made him so self-dependent that he had no pity to give to someone like herself, who had accepted the protection of strangers because she felt so lost and lonely . . . and scared.

Her head fell back sleepily against a cushion and worn out by the events of the day she drifted off to sleep. The room was in darkness when she awoke and she uncurled her stiff body and groped her way to the light switch. She blinked as the light came on, and was in the middle of a stretch when she noticed that Maryam had brought back her altered dress and laid it carefully across the foot of the bed.

Evening slippers of dark blue brocade had been put out for her, and with bated breath she slipped her feet into them. She gave a sigh of relief, and then wondered why it should cross her mind that they might be too small or too large for her. How odd of her! Your feet didn't alter in size because you lost a little weight.

She had a wash, then slipped into the pleated chiffon dress and studied her reflection in the mirror of the *armoire*. The soft draping of the dress was kind to the angularity of her body; the grey of her eyes picked up hints of blue from the material, and she had obeyed Madame's injunction to be more lavish with her lipstick. She didn't look too bad, she supposed, and then she saw her nose wrinkling up as she remembered the way Isabela Fernao had giggled when Duane had made his crack about the Sleeping Beauty.

'Rats!' she muttered. 'I don't like you either, Mr. Hunter!'

She turned from the mirror in a brisk swirl of chiffon and clicked off the light as she marched out of the room.

The corridor was lighted at intervals by wall-lamps, and vaulted overhead so that the effect was that of a cool, winding cloister. Set here and there were oval-shaped doors of varying colours, leading into bedrooms similar to her own, Roslyn conjectured. She thought the idea of coloured doors sensible as well as attractive, for it ruled out the mischance of a guest entering the wrong room.

Roslyn was approaching an arcade at the very end of the corridor when it occurred to her that on leaving her room she should have gone left instead of right. She was about to turn and remedy her mistake, when she noticed to one side of the fretted arch a narrow flight of steps leading upwards. She hesitated, then couldn't resist mounting them to find out if they led to the roof.

They did! She was out under the Arabian stars that pierced a smoke-grey sky, and with a little murmur of delight she went to the edge of the parapet and saw that from here the house faced the desert, awesome and shadowed, filled with a silence that yet held small sounds. The rustle of the long-leaved palm trees, the distant yap of a jackal, and the rumble of Arabic down in one of the courtyards.

Roslyn breathed the spicy night air of El Kadia, and felt in tune with the mystery and emptiness which lay for miles beyond the plantation . . . she seemed to belong here, and guessed that Armand had talked often about his family and Dar al Amra.

Suddenly her left hand clutched the parapet and the big diamond of Armand's ring shone like a tear in the starlight. It all came rushing back over her as she stared down at the ring she had been holding so tightly when the rescue squad had found her, flung yards from the wreckage of the big jet, with hardly a rag left to her back.

'Now don't get in a panic,' she warned herself, but still it came, that awful shaking that made her cling tightly to the tower wall of Dar al Amra.

'I'm Roslyn – Roslyn Brant,' she whispered as the terror of her plight swept over her. 'I'm twenty-two and I work for an airline and live in England . . .'

Perhaps she ought to return to England, to familiar places which might help her to find her way out of this blank, dark tunnel . . .

'Good evening – Juliet,' said a voice behind her.

Her heart contracted, then she swung round and saw a tall figure outlined against the star-grey sky. By a trick of the shadows the man's lower face seemed masked . . . but she would have known those keen, glinting eyes anywhere!

CHAPTER THREE

ROSLYN stood by the parapet, still as a hunted creature, as Duane Hunter drew near and towered beside her in the semi-darkness. 'Why – did you call me Juliet?' Her voice came back with a rush.

'I couldn't resist it,' he drawled. 'The balcony scene ah, but you wouldn't remember, I'm forgetting that you've lost your memory.'

'That was a cruel remark, Mr. Hunter.' Roslyn's hand clenched on the crenellated parapet. 'But then, if this household has to have an Inquisitor to find out if I'm faking my amnesia, I can understand them choosing you.'

He smiled through narrowed eyes, and it seemed to Roslyn that the shadows all around had somehow grown menacing. 'Why did you jump so, when I called you Juliet?' he crisped.

'Because you meant it as a shot in the dark, Mr. Hunter.' She met squarely his challenge of a glance. 'From the moment we met, you decided not to like me. You think me a plain nonentity whom your handsome cousin could never have been attracted to. But love is a funny thing—'

'The biggest joke perpetrated against mankind,' he agreed dryly.

'And I suppose you think if you wear an armour of cynicism, you'll escape Cupid's arrow?' For some intangible reason she was suddenly aware of enjoying herself, of being alive to the fact that though the plane crash had impaired her memory, it had not scattered her wits.

Duane Hunter leaned his back against the parapet, and Roslyn felt the rake of his eyes. 'As Isabela said, you speak up for yourself, my fey friend.' His voice was silky, dangerous. 'Quick wits are an indication of a mind on the alert rather than in a fog, so let me warn you, *Roslyn Brant*, that if you're playing a game with us, you'll be made to pay up in a way you won't like. Nanette is an open-hearted woman, and I won't see her led up the garden by some little chit who sees her as a soft touch, someone to provide free board and lodging, not to mention other perquisites.'

Roslyn felt slapped by the things he said, and she wanted to slap back, hard. Even as her hand itched, she hung on to her dignity and swung round to walk away from him. Swiftly he clamped a restraining hand on her arm and gave a pull that jerked her back against the parapet. Close to him, the grey tussore of his suit crushing her dress, she was very conscious of his lithe, disciplined strength. Her eyes dwelt wildly on his lean face, that was without a hint of humility.

'Why didn't you slap me, Miss Innocent-Eyes?' he mocked.

'I wouldn't lower myself to fight with a bully,' she said coldly.

At once he pressed her to the crenellated wall and came closer, his muscular warmth, his possible intention, making her shrink back until she was in real danger of tumbling through the parapet opening. He gazed down at her, his teeth glimmering in a smile of pure diablerie. 'You're quick with the verbal comeback,' he taunted. 'Now let me see you wriggle out of your present contretemps.'

She obliged by aiming a kick at his shin, forgetting that she wore soft brocade slippers and that his shin would be as hard as the rest of him. 'Oh – *you*! How dare you treat me like this?' she gasped, half in pain from a stubbed toe, and half in helpless rage.

'It must be the influence which this part of the house still exerts, ' he told her, enjoying her struggles. 'This is the harem tower.'

'Really?' She stood ruffled but interested as he let her go, her eyes straying round the tower and a little shiver running over her. So much had happened long ago in this desert house. Shades of the intrigue and the violence, the loving and the hating must linger to cast their shadows.

'Old houses are always haunted,' Duane said casually. 'It's part of their charm.'

Roslyn took a quick look at his face. Was he now trying to frighten her? she wondered. 'I don't think I'm frightened of ghosts,' she retorted. 'Least of all those of Dar al Amra. Armand lived here most of his life, and I—'

There she broke off and turned to gaze out over the desert, a sea of shadowed amber, with Dar al Amra an island upon which she had been cast up ... stormdrift ... which the man beside her was ready to cast back into the unknown.

'Does the desert frighten you?' The question came suddenly from Duane Hunter.

'If I said no, you'd smile with all the cynical superiority of a man who knows the desert in its worst moods,' she replied. 'I'm fascinated, Mr. Hunter, by what I've so far seen of it.'

'Fascination is the correct term,' he allowed. 'After four years I'm not certain whether I love its moods, or hate them. I sometimes think I like the desert best when it is wild, untamed, like a horse to be broken, or a woman.'

'I get a strong impression that you don't care very much for women, Mr. Hunter.'

'Women, say the Bedouins, were created from the sins of Satan.'

'And men are angels, I suppose?' she flashed back at him.

'As a matter of fact,' she caught the chatoyant gleam of his eyes, 'bachelors are called the brothers of the Devil.'

An appropriate term, she thought tartly, for the tower of gall and whipcord beside her. 'Which do you prefer, the desert or the jungle?' she asked.

'So,' he gave her a sideglance of lazy sarcasm, 'you've been warned that I learned my uncouth ways in the jungle?'

'Madame Gerard told me. I didn't realize at the time that she might be *warning* me against you.'

'You know better now?' he drawled.

'I know the worst,' Roslyn said, fingering a bruise on her upper arm. 'What sort of plantation did you supervise out in the jungle?'

'Rosewood, wild rubber, pineapples and coffee,' he listed.

'Do you prefer being a date planter?'

'In some ways,' he agreed. 'This is Gerard property and I am a Gerard. Whatever effort I put into the place is ploughed back into our pockets mainly, and I can enjoy a sense of personal victory and gain when we reap a particularly good harvest of fruit, or when a new idea of mine proves successful.'

'I should imagine that Dar al Amra is more attractive altogether than a plantation surrounded by bush and subject to torrential rains every so often,' Roslyn remarked.

Duane Hunter's eyes narrowed to that chatoyant glint that was so unnerving. 'How come you know such geographical facts, and yet lay claim to having no recollection of personal matters?' he demanded.

'The doctor at the hospital explained that it was one of the mysteries of amnesia,' she was on the defensive at once. 'I'm not playing a part, Mr. Hunter. My mind *is* a blank as far as personal matters are concerned ... my engagement to your cousin is real to me only because I wear his ring.'

Duane's eyes raked her face, then deliberately he

turned to a mass of flowers cloaking the wall beside them, creamy blooms with hidden hearts. He plucked one and ruthlessly forced back the petals in order to expose the hidden heart. Roslyn watched him and it seemed to her that the gesture was a threat. Then he tossed the broken flower over the parapet, took her by the arm and said curtly that it was time they were joining the dinner party.

Did he always come up to Dar al Amra for dinner? she wondered, feeling the tautness of her face, and the controlled pressure of his fingers about her arm. She hoped he didn't! She hoped very much that she wouldn't have to see Duane Hunter more than was unavoidable.

The dining room at Dar al Amra was as unconventional as its occupants, for they ate at small tables set in front of banquettes. Roslyn was companioned by Madame Gerard, very elegant in prune-coloured lace. Isabela was seated between the two men.

Her eyes were dramatically tinted, her dress the *vin rosé* of her lips, from out of which came wit, laughter and mockery in equal doses for her companions. Roslyn couldn't help watching the vivacity of her head and hand movements, the Moorish lamplight catching the jewelled arrow that secured her dark hair in a rich chignon.

'Nanette, how kind of you to give me two men to dine with,' she carolled from the other table. 'But why did you not keep one of them for the amusement of yourself – and little Roslyn, of course.'

'I am a rather wicked old woman, Isabela.' Nanette dabbed at her lips with her napkin and took a sip of Chinon *blanc* from her green *flute*. 'I could not be sure which of my grandsons you would prefer to torment tonight, so I decided to let them share you.'

Isabela had the laugh of a coloratura soprano and it rang out in that Moorish room. 'Yes, you are a little wicked, *chère madame*. 'You have lived so long in the

37

East that you have absorbed its polygamous attitudes.'

'Perhaps I have absorbed a great deal of the East.' Nanette smiled at Roslyn, and indicated with a very Gallic gesture that she drink her wine. 'I have lived at El Kadia for close on fifty years. I have seen it in war and peace, and now when I go to Paris I feel almost a stranger.'

'Paris will never completely forget Nina Nanette,' Tristan said gallantly, and turning towards his grandmother he raised his *flute* of wine. 'To you, Nanette, always *du chien*.'

'*Merci*, Tristan.' Her blue eyes softened, then flashed in challenge to Duane. 'And what do you say, *mon brave*? Have you a gallantry to offer your old grandmother?'

'You will never grow old while your eyes stay blue as a girl's,' he replied, in his laziest voice.

Roslyn heard Nanette catch her breath, then she inclined her snow-blue head to her half-English grandson and continued with her meal. Their first course was a spiced soup called *chorba,* and Roslyn was glad to resort to her wine every now and again.

'The shop windows of Paris are like stage-settings,' Isabela remarked. 'This dress I am wearing was bought there.'

'The dress becomes you, Doña Sol, but then you would look sexy in sackcloth,' Duane said mockingly. 'How are the aches and pains of your early morning gallop? Have they subsided yet?'

'I wonder that you have the nerve to ask, you barbarian.' Isabela studied his hard, brown face with her head on one side. 'You have not any sentiment in you,' she accused.

Bravo Isabela for saying it, Roslyn thought, her glance flicking the tropical grey worsted that made Duane Hunter look armoured in steel. He was gazing at the Portuguese girl with a half-smile on his lips, and the coppery lights in his eyes made them look less green and menacing than they had looked up on the harem tower.

The *babouches* of Jakoub and an Arab youth rustled across the carpet as they brought in the second course, shoulder of gazelle with a herb stuffing and a garnishing of vegetables in season. The Arab boy came to Roslyn's side and proffered the dish of vegetables. She raised her grey eyes to smile her acceptance ... and the smile froze on her lips at the sharp way he backed away from her, almost dropping the dish in his haste. He muttered something, and Roslyn, distressed, was conscious of Duane Hunter's piercing glance. He rapped out something in Arabic and the boy sullenly held out the dish for Roslyn, whose hands were trembling as she took a small helping of vegetables. She couldn't understand the boy's reaction. It hurt and bewildered her.

'It is all right, my child.' Nanette gave her hand a pat as the servants departed. 'Arabs are very superstitious, but you will grow used to their ways.'

'Superstitious?' Roslyn was still mystified by the incident.

'It's your eyes,' Duane said curtly. 'Grey eyes are regarded with mistrust by the Arabs.'

Roslyn flinched at the way he said it, then she bent her head over her plate and tears stung her eyes. She blinked hard and managed to subdue them, but the urge to run out of this house was not so easy to control. Her fork carried food to her mouth and she chewed automatically without tasting a thing. Isabela gave her a long stare of open curiosity, then conversation was resumed again, a buzz of voices to Roslyn who felt awkward, and hurt. She wished fiercely that she had not accepted Madame Gerard's offer of hospitality. She felt she couldn't stay here and decided to tell Nanette in the morning that she wanted to return to England.

Coffee was served in the *salon* by Jakoub, and Roslyn

sat down on a hassock to drink hers. She felt shielded by her decision to leave Dar al Amra in the morning; whatever was said, or thought, would not matter if she didn't have to stay here.

Tristan approached her with a small glass of cognac. 'Shall I tip it into your coffee?' he smiled. 'The two together are a splendid tonic.'

She liked Tristan, who looked so much like poor Armand, and she held out her cup and breathed the aroma of the cognac as it sank golden into the dark coffee. 'There,' Tristan said, 'drink that up and all your cares will steal away.'

'Thank you, *m'sieur*,' she smiled up at him.

'You are welcome, *mademoiselle*.'

She watched Tristan walk to the piano, then became aware that his cousin was watching her through the smoke of the cheroot he had just lighted. Dark brown, and lethal as himself! She took a gulp at the potent contents of her coffee cup, and felt reckless enough a minute later to gaze openly at Tristan, so Gallic and good-looking in his immaculate dinner jacket.

'Would you like me to play something for you?' Tristan was gazing directly back at her. 'You look like a squirrel, Roslyn—' and he ran his hands along the keys, producing a gay, woodsy tune that finally scampered up and up, as though into the shielding greenery of a tree.

Roslyn laughed, cognac-happy she supposed, but Isabela was not going to be left out of the limelight for very long, and with a rustle of *vin rosé* silk she joined Tristan at the piano. 'That is very quaint,' she said to him, 'but for the love of music play something that has depth, drama, emotion.'

'In other words, play something which Isabela can sing,' he mocked. 'What will it be, my diva?'

Though Isabela was vain and even a little malicious, Roslyn had already heard enough of her voice to know it was a thrilling one, and she felt a tingle of anticipation as the singer and the composer fell into a lively discussion about the aria she should sing. There was the song of the Tartar maiden in *Prince Igor,* which she had always adored. Then she shook her head and fell into the demure pose of Iris, the kidnapped *mousmé.*

'Not quite in character,' Duane called out, his dark face expressing a lazy enjoyment in the pantomime. 'Delilah or Salome would suit you much better.'

At once before their eyes she became Salome. The scene, she informed them, was the moment when King Herod sees Salome in the moonlight kissing the lips of the severed head of Joknaan the Prophet. She approached a table on which stood a platter of fruit, bent over it and turned round, a rose and green melon in her hands. Roslyn heard Duane chuckle to himself; his eyes through his cheroot smoke were drowsily content as a big cat's.

A few Moorish lamps cast pools of tinted light and shadow about the room, and Isabela stood half in shadow as she sang to them, the rather shallow person that she was submerged in the deep glory of her coloratura voice.

Roslyn listened with her arms clasped round her knees, cold little bumps rising on her skin as the finale of the song was reached and the ensuing silence was broken as they applauded Isabela's performance. It was then found that the content of the song had somehow set the mood for a discussion about that many-sided emotion called love. 'It is, I suppose, next to death the biggest drama in our lives,' Tristan swung round from the piano to survey everyone with a mournful smile touched with mischief. 'Love, I mean. Love, the cruel. Love the dénouement, the end that promises more.'

'Like old brandy, love must be enjoyed slowly.' Nanette's hands were cupping an inhaler, her smile was a little mysterious. 'I gaze into this glass – brandy glasses are a little like witch-balls, are they not? – and I see again the mistakes I made long ago, the heartaches I caused myself because being young I was also wilful. But for me all that is passed, and I can do nothing about the mistakes you four young people will make in your turn.'

'Come, Nanette, your happiness with *grandpère* was proverbial.' Tristan rose and went over to a smoking table to help himself to a cigarette. Duane extended a light and the eyes of the cousins met briefly.

'Happiness, like the aroma of cognac, is at its strongest when the bowl stands empty,' their grandmother said tartly. 'Happiness is an after-taste, too heady at the time to be appreciated by more than the senses. Inevitably a *mémoire du coeur.*'

'I want happiness right now,' Isabela said, with a prima donna outthrowing of her lovely arms. 'I demand that life give me everything while I am young.'

'Life will oblige in many respects, and it will also cheat,' Nanette said, with a wicked little chuckle. Then her blue glance pierced the man who faced her on a divan. 'What do you have to say about all this, *mon brave*? Cynicism is sometimes a shield for a romantic heart, though in your case I have my doubts.'

Duane Hunter had taken a peach from the side platter of fruit, and he was looking quizzical as he broke the peach in half and removed the stone at its heart. 'A peach, I think, would have been a much more symbolic fruit for Eve to have plucked,' he drawled. 'Soft and enticing on the outside, but just look at this!'

He held up the large stone, then tossed it into an ash-tray and bit into the fruit with careless enjoyment.

'Where did you learn to be so cynical?' Nanette spoke sharply, as though his action with the peach stone had really hurt her. 'What happened to you out in the green hell which used to be your home? Was it a woman, Duane?'

'Does it always have to be a woman?'

Roslyn flicked a glance at him as he wiped his fingers on a large white handkerchief, and she noticed how the lamplight cast his profile in copper and showed its taut, rather cruel lines.

'You are all Latin, Nanette, and so you see everything in terms of the eternal battle of the sexes,' he said lazily. 'I am neither a true Latin, nor a real Britisher. The traits of each are at war in me, and if I am a cynic, then I was born that way.'

'I wonder?' His grandmother was giving him an old-fashioned look. 'Remind me to have a long private talk with you one day, *mon brave*. No grandson of mine should be so devoid of the romantic spirit as you appear to be.'

'A romantic I might not be,' he grinned, 'but I always enjoy long private talks with beautiful women.'

Nanette smiled and played a moment with her rings, then she looked directly at Roslyn. 'Ah, *pauvre petite*, it has been a long day for you and those eyes of grey are barely able to keep sleep at bay. *Allons*, let you and me be off to our beds!'

Duane rose at once and helped his grandmother to her feet. He towered over her, the kind of man, Roslyn thought, who seemed stamped with a hard maturity that had come to him as a boy. She could not for the life of her visualize him as a child; but a picture of Tristan in a sailor suit sprang easily to her mind.

'Continue with your party, *mes enfants*,' Nanette smiled at Isabela and the two men. '*Bonne nuit*.'

'*Bonne nuit*,' Roslyn echoed, glancing round at the trio, Isabela lounging with grace among the cushions of a divan, Tristan propped in his dark attractiveness against the grand piano, Duane armoured in his steel-grey. Tristan alone smiled at her.

She parted from Nanette at the blue door of her room,

43

and took along to her own bedroom an impression of fragile porcelain, cleverly tinted but lined with age and the threat of a sudden breaking-up. Saying good-bye to Nanette would be hard, but Roslyn had made up her mind to leave Dar al Amra before the place laid its spell upon her . . . before the desert all around began to call to her.

Her Arab bed was strange but comfortable, and she laid a long time beneath its netting listening to the cicadas and the tick of the clock on her night table.

It was very late, she surmised, when she heard good-nights being exchanged down in the Court of the Veils. 'Who was she, Duane?' The voice of Isabela Fernao floated upwards and in through the harem lattices of Roslyn's room. 'Was she very attractive, this woman who made your heart so hard?'

'She's someone I never talk about.' Then he added in a gentler tone, 'Goodnight, Doña Sol. You must sing to me again some time.'

Footfalls echoed across the tiles of the courtyard, then they died away into the night, under the palms, while somewhere in the desert an animal howled mournfully.

Roslyn hoisted herself on an elbow and plumped the big, square pillow over the sausage bolster and settled down again. Her first day out of hospital had been a long, eventful one and though she felt so tired, sleep was proving very elusive tonight. She just couldn't stop thinking about the Gerards and seeing in her mind their striking faces, which the turbulent history of the family had modelled into lines of distinction and authority.

That history included the Reign of Terror, the tumbrel and guillotine. Soldiers who had explored the Sahara and fought in it; planters who had set up outposts of civilization. Women who had been headstrong and lovely . . .

The woman in Duane Hunter's jungle past had been like that, Roslyn thought sleepily. Lovely . . . the type

44

who broke hearts and left them ravaged by bitterness. Those that healed were never the same as before, a hardness set in, along with a distrust of women that was probably insurmountable.

Roslyn's eyelids grew heavy and her lashes settled into stillness on her cheeks. When the desert prowler came and howled a little closer to the walls of Dar al Amra, Roslyn was sleeping like a baby.

CHAPTER FOUR

ROSLYN awoke as the desert sun burst into life against the tawny walls of Dar al Amra. She had grown used in hospital to a bed swathed in netting, but not to seeing the sun filtering through harem lattices, and for a moment she couldn't think where she was.

Then it came to her, this was the desert domain of the Gerard family. Madame Gerard had brought her here yesterday. She lay a moment, letting the events of yesterday pass one after the other through her mind, then she sat up and pushed aside the tent-like netting.

Nanette would be annoyed, even a little hurt by her decision to leave Dar al Amra. She would be bound to say that Roslyn had given herself very little time to settle down here and grow used to the ways of the Gerards. If there were only *two* Gerards for her to grow used to, but there was a third, a man she would never like, or be liked by. Somehow he made it impossible for her to remain a guest in this desert house.

She slipped out of bed and wandered in bare feet to the nearest window. The sun stroked her neck and her bare arms and she gave a shiver of catlike pleasure at the warm touch of the sun, the hint of spice in the morning air. Somehow she knew that the life she had forgotten had held very little sunshine. She had been reared in an orphanage, and later on her home had been a hostel. Though her job had been that of an air hostess, flying schedules would not have given her much chance to explore the various stopping places. Airfield canteens would be all she saw of far-distant places.

The sun was warm and beguiling, and on impulse she ran into the bathroom to brush her teeth and have a wash.

She felt an urge to take a walk, and the courtyard below was empty but for the flutter of pigeons and other birds.

Back in her room she opened the clothes closet and selected a pair of tansy-gold pants and a cream cotton shirt, which fitted rather loosely because of her loss of weight but felt cool against her skin. She gave her hair a vigorous brushing, decided that it was not yet hot enough for a hat and hurried out eagerly to explore the Court of the Veils.

The young are all part of nature and Roslyn – quite unaware – blended with the early morning freshness of the trees and flowers of the courtyard as she wandered about among them. Roses clustered and swarmed with bees, swinging out from a trellis on a warm breeze. There was a bush of white camellias, stunning things that would have cost quite a price in a florist's shop, plumed violet jacarandas, and trim scented junipers. The fountains had not yet been turned on and they stood shaded by the great charmed tree that might have been a weeping pepper.

Roslyn reached up a hand to touch the jade leaves, renewed each year on this tree which had stood like a guardian of the court throughout its long history. Here and there the walls had small slots in them, and when Roslyn put her eye to one of them and it looked directly into the room that was now the *salon*, she guessed that the slots had been used by the eunuchs to spy on the girls of the harem. There they would have lounged about on cushions, tinkered with their jewellery, gossiped and eaten the sweets and sherbets that made them so plump and appealing to the Moslem male.

Roslyn frowned to herself, recalling the gleam of suspicion in Duane Hunter's eyes last night. But it *was* odd, the way her mind yielded all this schoolbook trivia while obstinately refusing to give up the essential personal facts that seemed buried in some lost pocket of her mind.

She lifted a hand to feel through her growing hair the scar where she had been stitched up in hospital. It was about an inch long and was still a little puckered about the edges. That was why she had to use a hairbrush instead of a comb, in case the teeth of the comb tore the edges of her scar.

She sighed and stood gazing pensively at the weeping pepper tree, the thought of poor Juliet Grey coming into her mind.

Her heart missed a beat. Why had that Hunter man called her Juliet? Whatever did he think, that she was pretending to be his dead cousin's fiancée? It wasn't possible anyway, a deception like that. The crash had been investigated by officials from England; they said she was Roslyn Brant ... then there was the ring. She had been clutching Armand's diamond ring in her hand when the rescue team found her and rushed her to hospital with the other few survivors. Two of those had died in hospital, the third, a business man, had gone home to England before Roslyn was fit enough to be allowed out of bed.

She gave a cold little shiver as she remembered waking up in hospital to pain and loss of self. She hadn't known her name, and that had been the worst feeling of all, until they addressed her as Roslyn and a distinct sense of familiarity had come to her. Yes, she had nodded eagerly, I know that name!

Lost in her thoughts, Roslyn opened a slave gate in the wall of the courtyard and wandered through it. There came stealing back into her mind that remark of Duane Hunter's heard under her window last night; his curt confession to Isabela that there had been another woman in his life, one he never talked about. It was she who had made him cynical towards all other women; amazingly he must have loved her if she had managed to scar a heart as hard as his.

Duane Hunter in love was a picture Roslyn couldn't imagine. Even his response to the seductive Isabela held tinges of mockery.

The Court of the Veils had been filled with sunshine, now Roslyn became aware of a cloister-like coolness and she saw that she was walking beneath the giant fans of the Dar al Amra date-palms. Great pendants of desert fruit hung among leaves almost as tall as herself, and alongside her path she could hear toads croaking in the irrigation ditches, and overhead the cawing of birds in the tall trees.

Half-bewitched, she wandered on, barely noticing that the aisles between the rows of trees were all alike, flecked with strange green shadows and offering no guide to a stranger of the way out of the plantation. She caught no glimpses of cowled workers, as she had in the car yesterday, and was quite unaware that the plantation extended to fifty square miles and that today the men were busily at work in another section of this vast network of date, sago, oil, and betel-nut palms.

Her keenest awareness was that the smells all around were musky and heady, everything was quiet but for the hidden toads and birds, not for weeks had she felt such a sense of peace.

Some time later she saw something gleaming among the trees, a stream coursing through the cool silence of the palm forest with grass and flowers growing on its banks. She knelt in the grass and scooped the clear water into the palms of her hands. Her throat was dry, and she drank thirstily, and dabbed her temples and nape with her moist hands. Mmmm, that felt good, and sitting back on her heels she took stock of her surroundings.

The sky through chinks in the fans overhead was a brilliant blue streaked with honey, and the down-stabbing lances of sunlight were hot as they touched her. The sun of early morning had blossomed into its desert lushness, which meant that she had been wandering in these 'wild woods of Hella' for some time.

I ought to start back, she thought, but it was so peaceful here. A squirrel with a dark-striped back and a large bushy tail darted up a palm trunk and made her think of Tristan's quaint little tune last night. A toad hopped out of the stream, went still as a stone and peered at her with huge eyes of topaz. She felt at one with these forest creatures, and resting on the banks of the stream she studied her drowned reflection in the water.

'Mirror, mirror, in the woods,' she murmured with a smile. 'Should I stay, or run away?'

The water rippled, as though touched by a cat's paw. The furrow at the nape of her neck went strangely cold ... she twisted round where she sat and saw a few yards away a sleek, cat-like creature staring at her with baleful green eyes. Her blood seemed to go to ice, for its tail was lashing back and forth and it looked as though it was getting ready to spring at her. Its top lip drew back and bared wicked-looking fangs, it spat and gave a snarl as Roslyn leapt to her feet.

'Stand quite still!' a voice rapped out.

And Roslyn stood petrified as something as sleek as the cat launched itself from among the trees and landed square on the back of the snarling feline. In an instant the air was filled with the rage of the battling animals, spitting, ripping, rolling over and over until they fell with a splash in the stream and the big cat eluded its attacker and fled away, leaving a lean, long-legged dog to shake itself on the banks of the stream.

'Good lad, Hamra!' A hand slapped the wet, reddish coat of the dog, and Roslyn, her heart still pounding in the vicinity of her throat, watched as Duane Hunter looked the dog over and pronounced him scratched but otherwise unhurt.

'It was a good thing you both c-came along when you

did,' she said shakily.

'You shouldn't be wandering about here as though you were taking a stroll through Middlesex,' he snapped. 'Mountain cats and wild dogs come down from the hills now and again, and you stood a very good chance just now of getting badly mauled.'

'I know.' She flinched from the cut in his voice, and turned for relief to the lean dog who had come a little closer to her and was snuffing her sandals. She gave him a pat and at once he backed away from her.

'A Saluki isn't a pet dog,' Duane Hunter said crisply. 'He's a hunter.'

'An appropriate companion for you,' she retorted, flashing a glance over the dark fire of his hair, down his haughty blade of a face to the bark-brown throat bared by his white shirt. His breeches were latched into knee-boots of Moroccan leather.

'I see you are now over your fright.' Something gleamed in his eyes. 'Do you mind telling me what you are doing so far from the house?'

'No, I don't mind.' She thrust her hands into the pockets of her pants and tilted her chin in the air. 'I felt like a walk before breakfast and it was so cool and peaceful under the palms that I lost track of time.'

'And direction, I don't doubt.' He snapped his fingers and the Saluki bounded towards him. 'You'd better come and have some coffee and something to eat at my place. Then I'll take you back to Dar al Amra.'

She gulped, none too sure that she wanted to accept his invitation. 'Come on!' He was striding away among the trees with Hamra loping along in front of him. Roslyn hesitated, then followed, brushing bits of grass from her pants. When he shot a look over his shoulder and paused so that she could catch up with him, she felt like running away.

'I believe I scare you more than that cat did,' he jeered.

51

'You're about as uncivilized,' she rejoined breathlessly, for she was striving to keep up with his free desert stride.

'I am not *très sympathique* like Tristan, eh?' He laughed, and here in these palm-green aisles it sounded extra deep and relishing, and caused a shaft of small bright birds to fly out in alarm from among the dense foliage.

'Tristan takes after Nanette, who is the very best of women,' he said. 'Gracious, witty, with too much heart to break.'

'She is very kind,' Roslyn agreed, a catch in her voice because it would hurt, leaving Nanette. 'Her visits to me in hospital were more than welcome and I—'

'You are in a position to hurt her, and you had better not!' His glance flashed downwards, copper green, almost as menacing as the baleful glare of that mountain cat.

She couldn't drag her eyes from his, agleam with a narrow smile. 'There were two Kilkenny cats,' he drawled, 'who fought until only their tails were left.'

'Is that how it's going to be if I stay at Dar al Amra?' she shot back at him.

'Inevitably – Miss Brant.'

They stopped walking, as if by mutual consent, and faced each other beneath the towering palms. Her eyes lifted to his face were the colour of grey jade in this light. 'I think I had better leave Dar al Amra,' she said.

'No.' He shook his head. 'I won't have Nanette hurt in any way. You'll stay as long as my grandmother wants you to. You'll stay because she has lost Armand – because of *this*.'

And before Roslyn could elude him, he shackled her left wrist with his hard fingers and lifted her hand so that a streak of sunlight fired the big diamond. 'Nanette cherished three rings which were given to her by her husband,' he said deliberately. 'When Tristan, then I, and finally Armand reached the age of twenty-one, we each received one of those rings to give in our turn to a woman we wished to marry. You wear Armand's ring without a shadow of doubt in the world. The inscription inside was put there by my grandfather, for that was how he felt about Nanette, that they would always be together in life and death.'

'And you refuse to believe that Armand could have felt the same way about me?' she said quietly.

Silence spun a web about them as he studied her upraised face. Then a bird cawed and Roslyn attempted to pull free of the fingers about her wrist. It was impossible. They were steely as his eyes, obstinate as his chin, cruel as his mouth.

'It isn't for me to judge Armand's taste in women,' he drawled.

'Yet you are judging me, Mr. Hunter. You think me plain, which I admit is true, but not all men are attracted by a jay bird, some prefer a jenny-wren.'

With a lift of a satirical brow, he caught at her chin with his free hand and turned her face from left to right. 'No, you're not a beauty,' he agreed coolly, 'but neither are you a jenny-wren. A chameleon is a better name.'

'A chameleon changes from one moment to the next,' she said indignantly.

'So it does.' His fingers gripped her chin, then let go, and a minute later they emerged from the green gloom of the plantation and were confronted by the arched entrance of his Moorish house. The Saluki gave a bark and bounded off across the patio, disappearing through an archway that led indoors.

It was a house built from blocks of desert stone, with an air of mystery about it, Roslyn thought, as she stepped under the patio entrance stamped with the Hand of Fate.

Fate was surely playing a game with her, leading her like a lamb into the lair of the wolf.

She glanced about her and saw tiles overlaid with coloured arabesques, ironwork seats, and some stone troughs of red geraniums, marigolds, blue irises and tall lilies – knights and their ladies – and cascades of aromatic wall creepers blending with the dragon's blood of the bougainvillea that half-concealed the whitewashed walls.

There were trees that towered above the house, shading it and also exposing it to the risk of lightning in a storm.

'Come indoors and have a glass of *abri*,' Duane said. 'It's about the most refreshing drink I know of.'

She walked beside him across the tiles and entered one of the rooms that, like all the others, faced the walled garden in a crescent. The house had no upper storey, only a flat roof with some lines of washing hanging still in the heat.

Roslyn caught her breath as she entered for the first time the barbaric den of Duane Hunter. The floor was decked with jungle pelts, the furniture was of cane, the lamps and pottery Moorish, while a big cedar recess was jammed with books, thrust in here and there with no attempt at neatness. Another cupboard with a glass front held several rifles; on a chest of carved cedarwood there stood a radiogram, and on a low table a musical box with a dancing girl on top of it.

This item caused Roslyn a jolt of speculation. It was out of tune with the rest of the room and made her wonder if it had belonged to the woman he never talked about.

'Take the weight off your feet while I get my boy, Da-ud, to fix us a couple of *abris* and some breakfast.'

Roslyn couldn't resist his ocelot-covered divan, and taking him at his word she curled up on it, along with her thoughts as Duane strode off to order their breakfast. She

54

felt primitive among the spotted pelts, brought from the jungle where the Hunter man had learned to be so self-sufficient, with the power to impose his will upon others and not care that he was feared or disliked for his strong will in a body of iron.

She didn't hear him come back into the room and she gave a little start as he moved, jungle lithe, across her line of vision. 'I see you take after Tristan in one respect,' she gestured at the radiogram. 'You appear to be fond of music.'

'It tames the savage breast,' he grinned down at her curled-up figure on the ocelot skins. 'Shall I put on a record while we eat our breakfast?'

'Have you any electricity?' she asked.

'Plenty.' His glance crackled with meaning. 'Dar al Amra has its own generator and my house benefits, naturally.'

'Naturally,' she murmured, her fingernails digging into the skins of the ocelots he had no doubt killed. 'You make sure you always get what you want, don't you?'

'Oh, there have been one or two occasions when I have been foiled.' He lifted back the lid of the radiogram and took a look at the record on the turntable. 'I'm not exactly modern-minded when it comes to music,' he said. 'This is one of my favourites, which I used to play a lot at our plantation in the rain forest. *Der Rosenkavalier.*'

'The Rose-Bearer.' She broke into a smile. 'You would come armed with a club.'

'No doubt,' he drawled. He switched on the Richard Strauss music, and lowered the volume so they could still talk. An iridescent dragonfly hummed into the room and they watched it circle the white walls. Its wings were magnetic as the flash of Duane Hunter's eyes.

'The male dragonfly is utterly ruthless towards its mate, you know,' he remarked. 'Out in the rain forest some of them were as big as birds.'

55

'Do you miss all that?' she asked. 'I detect a note of nostalgia in your voice.'

'It was my home,' he made a gesture that revealed the French blood in him, lean, burned a leathery brown, his eyes glinting like tourmalines in his face that could have belonged to a seventeenth-century corsair. 'Naturally Dar al Amra has provided compensations in that I am the head man of this outfit, that I have the desert to ride in, and fifty square miles of palms to cultivate and care for.'

'Fifty square miles!' she echoed. 'I had no idea the plantation was that immense.'

'Doubtless, from the way you were wandering about in it.' He bared his teeth in that mocking smile of his. 'It harbours snakes as well as an occasional cat. Scorpions too.'

'Are you warning me to keep out of your territory?' She regarded him with the gravity of a child who couldn't quite understand his attitude.

'Not specifically. But this isn't Epping Forest, and apart from snakes and scorpions there are the Arab workers.' His eyes raked her boyish figure from her throat to her heels. 'You are on the skimpy side, it's true, and they prefer a plump wench, but all the same you are a female and I can't be in a dozen places at once.'

'I am sure you try,' she said tartly. 'Anyway, what makes you think I'm going to stay at Dar al Amra?'

'You are, of course.'

'Because of the free board and lodging, not to mention other perquisites?'

'Sharp as a nail, aren't you?' That baffling gleam came and went in his eyes as he picked up from the bureau beside him a carving of a forest Indian arching his body to aim a spear. He ran his thumb over the wood that was already smooth and dark from much handling. 'Maybe you were planning to leave, but now you've breathed the desert I don't think you will. Primitive places can do that to some people, just as cities like Paris can enchant others.'

'You think the primitive is more likely to appeal to me?' The idea excited her deep down, and she forgot for a while how he had threatened her under the trees, his fingers biting into her wrist as Armand's diamond blazed between them.

'Time will tell,' he drawled, and in that moment *babouches* shuffled into the room and a lean youth in a *galabieh* and a red skull cap brought a tray to Roslyn. She took one of the frosted glasses of pink *abri* and met slanting eyes of *blue* above high cheekbones.

'El Rumh not often eating breakfast at home,' Da-ud informed her. 'I make *café noir* in a flask and giving him dates to eat under the trees.'

'I am sure El Rumh prefers that,' she said, looking wickedly demure as she cast a glance at the boy's master.

'This morning I am making liver kebabs with tomatoes and onions.' Da-ud lifted his snub nose and sniffed. 'It is all smelling pretty good, no?'

'It is all smelling very good indeed,' she smiled back at him.

'I'll have my *abri* before the ice melts.' Duane whipped his glass off the tray. 'Now hop off to the kitchen, pronto, before those kebabs turn into cinders.'

Da-ud hopped off with a grin that cut a white line in his brown face. 'He's a Berber,' Duane said in answer to Roslyn's inquiring look. 'They and the Arabs are two distinct peoples.'

'But like the Arabs you consider that grey eyes are not to be trusted.' Her ice-cooled drink had a delicious spicy taste.

'Eyes of grey stay away,' his look pierced her over the rim of his glass. 'They do have something a trifle mysterious about them. Maybe it's because they can catch the light, and also the shadows, like a deep lake.'

'I must go and see the Temcina Lake,' she said quickly,

heat in her cheeks. 'Why did your boy call you El Rumh?'

He shrugged carelessly. 'It's a name I have around these parts.'

'What does it mean?'

'I'll be darned if I'll tell you.' He laughed curtly and set aside his empty glass. 'You women are as inquisitive as horses.'

'How flattering!'

'I never flatter.' There was a twist to his mouth. 'It makes a woman look coy, and I dislike coyness.'

'I think you dislike quite a lot about women,' she dared to say.

'Like horses, I prefer those with a bit of temper in them.'

'The women rate second place, I notice.'

'Why not?' His face in that moment was as hard as teak. 'Women are too often less loyal than the horse, and though both are equally greedy for sugar, a horse can't sweet-talk a man into making an ass of himself.'

'That is your definition of a man in love, I take it, Mr. Hunter?'

'Take it whichever way you like, Miss Brant. Love is a fool's game, and if Armand hadn't got enticed into playing it, he'd have come home much sooner and would probably be alive today.'

Her face tightened with pain at his words. 'The Arabs say *In sha Allah*. Don't you believe that what is to be will be?'

'If all our little histories are already written,' he said cynically, 'then this whole shebang of a world is a puppet show, with you, me, and everyone else all dancing on the end of strings. I don't like that! I want to be the boss of my own fate.'

'You would "cleave the earth and equal the mountains"?' she half smiled. 'You're an arrogant man, and a rather frightening one, Mr. Hunter.'

'You carry plenty of sail for a cockleshell, Miss Brant.' He was beside the divan in a stride ... offering her a hand up, a grin on his lips.

'I thought you never flattered women.' Uncurled off the divan and standing in front of him, she had to put back her head to look at him, way above her, tough and tanned.

'I don't,' he jeered. 'Kids don't matter, and you look like one in pants, curled among those pelts of mine.'

'You certainly live up to your name,' she gestured round the room. 'Quite a few animals must have fallen to your gun.'

'The jaguar and leopard skins are off cats I killed,' he agreed mockingly. 'Both are killers for the sake of the kill, but the ocelot skins were a gift from a Jivaro chieftain. Does your store of remembered facts include the Jivaro and their main speciality?'

How sarcastic he could be! With her hand itching for contact with his jaw, she turned from him and went and stood in the archway that framed the walled garden. 'Your arrogant head would have made a redoubtable trophy,' she threw over her shoulder. 'I can't understand why the Jivaro weren't tempted.'

He laughed right behind her, and she stepped out quickly into the patio where Da-ud was laying the iron-work table for their breakfast. He flashed her a mischievous smile, which she answered absently. She didn't want to eat breakfast with Duane Hunter in his patio. She didn't like the man, and as Da-ud went indoors she swung round on Duane and saw him lounging against a palm trunk, crushing the bougainvillea at its base. 'You're so sure of yourself, aren't you?' she accused. 'Armoured against most of the pricks and pains felt by other people.'

'*Most* of the pricks and pains?' He cocked an eyebrow. 'Surely I'm immune to all of them?'

'I thought so, at first,' she fingered the cape of green

59

and mauve creepers, and added recklessly: 'It quite surprised me to hear that someone did manage to find a chink in your armour – a woman, I understand.'

The patio was hung with silence, then Roslyn's gasp was almost a cry as Duane's hands caught hold of her shoulders. 'Who told you that?' His face above her was a series of harsh, cold angles. 'Was it Nanette?'

'No-no—'

'Who, then?' He shook her and a strand of fair hair fell into her eyes. 'Come on, tell me!'

'I – I heard you telling Isabela – last night.' Roslyn was suddenly frightened of his touch, which bruised, and the copper flames in his green eyes. 'L-let me go – you're hurting me!'

It only hurt her all the more to struggle, and indignation blazed in her eyes when he said coldly: 'Didn't anyone ever teach you to respect the privacy of other people?'

'You should keep your voice down when you say good night to Isabela right under my window,' she fought back. 'I don't want to overhear the secrets you confide to her. I'm just not interested, or concerned because some woman caused you to become hard-boiled and cynical.'

Again there was that taut silence between them, so that the hidden chirr of cicadas and the trickle of water among the encircling trees seemed more persistent. Roslyn's heart was beating rapidly and though Duane Hunter's face was now deadly still, she could envisage the wince that had flicked across it a moment ago.

That wince of pain confirmed what she had thought last night ... he cared still for the woman he had known before he came to Dar al Amra.

CHAPTER FIVE

THE tension became a palpable humming, then Roslyn saw a ruby-throat go whirring by, gay as a kiddy's toy.

'Come, we had better eat our kebabs before they get cold.'

Duane let her go and she walked past him to the table, where Da-ud stood regarding them with slant-eyed interest. Roslyn slipped into the patio chair which Duane drew out for her with curt politeness, and as soon as they were both seated Da-ud, bursting with pride, whipped the domes off the plates set in front of them. *Le petit déjeuner est servi,*' he said, turning at once to Roslyn to add: 'You think, *lella,* I am speaking English and French pretty good?'

'As good as all this, Da-ud,' she smiled, gesturing at the liver kebabs with sections of onion and tomato, bread with a glistening crust, a rose of butter, and the jar of honey beside a mound of small fluffy doughnuts.

'You've excelled yourself, Da-ud,' Duane said approvingly.

Da-ud beamed all over his face and after pouring their coffee into brass-held cups, he plucked a fistful of marigolds and laid them beside Roslyn's plate. *'Bon appetit,'* he said in French, and backed off into the house with an Eastern salaam.

Roslyn laughed and fingered her posy, the bean-spiciness of the coffee mingling with the sun on trees and creepers. 'How charming,' she said meaningly.

'If a Berber or an Arab takes to you, then you've made a friend for life.' Duane informed her, forking kebab into his mouth. 'They can also be as heartless as vultures, and shrewd as Swiss bankers. I found Da-ud a couple of years ago working in the Berber hills, using a sling that whizzed stones at the birds who came after the sparse crops they managed to grow up there. He was half-starved, eager as anything to work for a European. Everything that comes to the table is native, and I'm afraid my guests have to put up with what is provided.'

'You're never afraid, Mr. Hunter,' she rejoined. 'Anyway, I'm enjoying every mouthful of Da-ud's cooking – this bread has an intriguing flavour!'

'It's semolina bread,' he informed her. 'Makes crunchy toast. We should have asked for some – shall I call the boy?'

She shook her head. 'I like it as it is, with butter.'

'D'you like your coffee?'

She nodded, and he refilled her cup. 'Well made Arab coffee is about the best,' he said. 'But take my advice and steer clear of mint tea. It's as horrible as it looks.'

'Then it's taken for granted that I'm staying at Dar al Amra,' she remarked in a while, her lips sticky and sweet from doughnut and honey.

'Nanette needs someone,' he said crisply. 'Be good to her, I'm warning you. She's the first woman in my life, and I can be hellishly angry on her behalf.'

'I'm sure you can.' Roslyn hid the sudden shake of her lips behind her table napkin. She was half annoyed again, half wounded. It wasn't a pleasant feeling to be under suspicion, even by the Hunter man who had a down on all women outside the magic circle that included only his grandmother and the lovely Latin whose golden voice seemed to tame his savage breast.

When the time drew near for him to take her home, he told Da-ud to get the stable-hand to saddle him a mount. One mount? Roslyn stiffened in her chair, her eyes fixed on Duane as he bent his head to fire a cheroot.

The sun struck full on his coppery hair as he blew a plume of strong smoke. 'Even if you could ride, I wouldn't trust you alone on one of my Barbs,' he drawled.

'Couldn't we walk?' she asked faintly.

'I've wasted enough valuable time this morning, Miss Brant.' He quizzed her through his cheroot smoke. 'There's no need to look apprehensive. Barbs are highly strung, but I'm quite proficient at handling them. What are you scared of?'

He knew all right! It was a relief when his Saluki came bounding to the table, still wary of her but not averse to the scraps of liver left from her breakfast.

The Barb was saddled and brought round to the patio. It was a glossy fawn colour with a dark-honey muzzle, sidling nervously until Duane approached and ran a soothing hand down the curving neck. He spoke to the horse in the Berber tongue, then he beckoned to Roslyn, who came to his side feeling less nervous of the spirited Barb than of its master.

'You'll add no more weight to Lekna's back than the cloak I wear for my evening gallops,' Duane said.

'Lekna? What a beautiful name for a horse.' Her hand was pale against the silky coat, then her fingers were clenching the dark mane as without warning Duane took hold of her and shot her on to the back of this animal with wicked ears close to its head and the speed of the wind in its every sinew. With a supple bound Duane was in the saddle behind her, his arms a muscular arc around her as he took the reins.

'All set?' he demanded.

She nodded, the breath knocked out of her throat at finding herself in his arms in this way, the wall of his chest against her lightly-clad shoulder, firm and alive with the vigour of the man.

The Barb broke into a canter and they passed under the patio archway and out among the date-palms. The green coolness swooped down like a wing, and Roslyn held herself rigid so as not to feel again the lift and fall

63

of Duane's chest. The *human* feel that rendered him less frightening and at the same time more unnerving ...

'H-how tall these trees are,' she said nervously.

'Thirty to forty feet,' he replied. 'The trees of life that grew in the Garden of Eve. Did you know that the date palm as to be "married" by human hand?'

'No,' she said, her eyes on the brown hand that held the reins in front of her.

'The male palm has about ten "brides" who yield fruit to him after pollination,' Duane went on. 'The date-palm bears its first fruit at eight years of age, and is mature at thirty. It yields for close on a century. Wonderful, eh?'

'A woman should be as clever,' she agreed pertly. 'No wonder you're in love with your trees.'

'No wonder.' He gave a short whiplash of a laugh. 'What woman could provide so well for a man for a hundred years? Fruit to subsist on, shade in the sun, a roof and bedding provided by its leaves and fibres. Everything – even peace of mind.'

'I shouldn't have thought that peace of anything appealed to you,' she said. 'Anyway, if the primitive offers peace, then women must also provide it to a certain extent. *We* are primitive, aren't we?'

'Primitive, but far more subtle than either the jungle or the desert,' he drawled.

'You said I should like the desert, Mr. Hunter. Did you mean it?'

'Why not?' His tone of voice was indifferent. 'You seemed on the harem tower last night to appreciate its mystery, its sense of the infinite that invites forgetfulness.'

It flashed across her mind that she had more than her share of forgetfulness to contend with already, but she held back from reminding him of the fact. To him her amnesia was like a red rag to a bull, and being this close to him drained her of fight, made her helplessly aware that his mercy would never be sweet.

'If you're keen to see something of the desert, I daresay Tristan could be persuaded to take you exploring.' He glanced down at her, and as it happened she was half turned to meet that glance. His face in the green light of the trees had something devilish about it; all that was untamed in the desert – *his* desert, which he didn't offer to show her – seemed reflected in his eyes as they met hers.

'Is Tristan fond of the desert?' she asked. 'Somehow he seems too sophisticated.'

'For all his city manners, Tristan has more illusions about places and people than I had even as a schoolboy,' came the dry reply. 'He's like his namesake, the Knight of Brittany. A gallant in search of a damsel in distress.'

'Anyone can see that Tristan is kind.' Roslyn was rigid with awareness of the arm that half encircled her, ridged with muscles whose steel was only inches from her body.

'And anyone can see that I am not.' His laughter brushed her nape, and even as she felt its warmth something in the path of the Barb caused it to rear suddenly and sharply into the air. Roslyn was pitched against Duane and his arm crushed her as he gripped the reins and forced the Barb back to a canter. His arm relaxed and as Roslyn caught her breath, he glanced down at her. 'Sorry,' he said curtly. 'Did I hurt you?'

She shook her head, and though his arm was now held away from her, she still felt the hard muscles straining into her softness.

The green shadows were gradually turning gold, and a few minutes later they came in sight of the lion-coloured walls of Dar al Amra. Relief was a taste in Roslyn's throat. She could hardly wait to escape from Duane Hunter.

'I'll drop you off just here,' he said, and the Barb was halted just short of a side entrance. Duane dismounted and gave her a hand down.

'Thank you for coming to my rescue, and for feeding me,' she said, her triangular eyes of rain-grey lifted to his face, her face here in the green-gold shadows that of a young and wistful witch.

'It was a mere stroke of luck that I came along with my dog.' A smile crisped the edge of his mouth, mocking and careless. 'Kismet, as they say here in this land of locusts and honey.'

'You don't believe in Kismet,' she reminded him.

'The Devil knows!' His wide shoulders lifted on a shrug. 'I am not constituted to accept, I want to *take*. And you, young Roslyn, are you woman enough to know that it is the basic difference between the sexes?'

His brows made a fierce, straight line, the flesh was close to the hard, thrusting bones of his face. His eyes were green as the palm leaves that lanced in the sun, narrow and glittering.

'I know that we shall fight whenever we meet,' she said. 'I have been warned.'

'Men and women are always at war with each other about something,' he drawled. 'Even in each other's arms they only recoup their energy for more fighting.'

'What a cynical outlook on life,' she chided him.

'I wasn't being entirely cynical,' he rejoined. 'Sex is a fundamental truth, but very few people like facing it. Instead they dress it up in all sorts of romantic garments, veils of illusion, disguising a basic drive as a dream. It is better to see things as they are, Miss Brant. Dreams are for those who want to be hurt.'

With that he turned from her and vaulted into the saddle of his Barb. He threw her a farewell salutation and as he wheeled his horse, man and mount were outlined vividly against the trees. Both were alive with a violence that made Roslyn retreat against a bush of flowers, some of which burst and shed musky petals over her shoulders and bare arms. Duane gave the Barb its head, and soon the pair were lost among the trees and their thunder died away into silence.

As Roslyn entered Dar al Amra, the slave gate gave a clang behind her. The lion-coloured walls all around were high . . . guarding the citadel where she must remain until the spell upon her was broken.

The Sleeping Beauty was awoken with a kiss, she thought, and with a sigh she sat down under the weeping-pepper tree and watched the fountains pulsing upwards, pluming into the sun. Well, whatever kind of person she had been before the crash, one thing was certain. She was deeply responsive to the things of nature. She felt more at ease among them than with people.

'. . . books in the running brooks. and good in everything.' Though her mind was divided territory, she remembered lines like that, but she could not tell Nanette about the happiness she must have felt with Armand . . . if she had loved him?

Love, the quiet delight that surges beneath the surface . . . the torrent that breaks its dams at high tide. The wonder, and the wild desire, they left their wounds, too deep for the heart or the soul's forgetting.

Yet she had forgotten what love had felt like, and so she must doubt that she had ever felt its full force. She shivered in the sun of the east, and knew a desperate yearning for the truth that was locked away in her mind, the key to it lost. She couldn't bear to think that she might be the kind to deceive a man . . . yet when Duane Hunter had talked about deception she had felt a curious sensation of guilt, as though subconsciously she knew his distrust of her to be justified.

Oh no! She jumped to her feet and ran from her thoughts to the comfort of Tristan and his music.

In the days that followed Roslyn didn't venture again into the palm groves, where she might meet Duane unexpectedly.

At breakfast time she joined Tristan and they feasted together on cold slices of melon, hot *croissants* and coffee. He always had plenty to talk about and they were fast becoming friends ... to Isabela's rather mocking amusement.

Isabela had also been invited to stay at Dar al Amra for as long as she wished. Just at present she had no operatic commitments, and being Portuguese she had a natural love of the Sun, and was always prepared to sing for Tristan whenever he wished her to.

They had become acquainted, he told Roslyn, when Isabella had sung in his opera *Ar Mor*, a legend of Brittany which he had set to music and which had proved his first big success on the operatic stage.

'I believe that is all the girl wants from my Tristan, the lovely arias he can compose for her,' Nanette said one morning to Roslyn, as the gorgeous sound of Isabela's singing echoed through the house. 'In a way I am glad. I should not wish a grandson of mine to waste himself on a girl wrong for him.'

Roslyn glanced up from Nanette's album of theatrical memories. She didn't think Tristan was in love, but his grandmother must think so or she wouldn't have spoken in that vein. 'One can understand the attraction,' Roslyn said casually. 'Isabela is stunning with her golden skin and dark hair.'

'Tristan feels an attraction for her, *petite*,' Nanette spoke from her *escritoire* where she was doing the household accounts, 'but you must have noticed that it is my desert barbarian who has caught her Latin eye?'

'Aren't you afraid of seeing *him* in her coils?' Roslyn bit back a smile and studied a photograph of Nanette in a tricorne hat trimmed with ospreys.

'*Mais non*,' Nanette gave the laugh that was curiously more robust than she looked. 'Duane can take care of himself in any situation, but Tristan is sensitive, an idealist. He might run away with the idea that Isabela has a nature to match her voice, but Duane is too canny to be fooled. Even should the girl succeed in leading him to the altar, it will be he who will take the lead for the rest of their lives. I *know*. I was the wife of his grandfather.'

'He is such a cynic about women.' Roslyn was gazing at Nanette wide-eyed. 'Do you really think there is a chance of him marrying Isabela?'

'Though a cynic about women, and therefore marriage, he will be obliged like other men to be a realist.' Nanette peered keenly at Roslyn over halfmoon spectacles. 'Only devils or saints can live alone, and though Duane is much of a devil, he is much more a man. A man who needs a woman to love and depend on him.'

'What of Isabela's career?' Roslyn asked. 'Do you think she would be prepared to give up the adulation of the crowd in order to live in the wilds? I am sure your grandson would never agree to live in a city.'

'The idea is amusing, isn't it?' Nanette chuckled and set aside her pen. 'Duane in a city would be like a lion in a cage. His grandfather would have been the same, that is why I gave up my career and came to Dar al Amra to live with him. I was even more famous than Isabela, you know. Those were the days of wit and wine and gallantry, and I adored them. The elegant clothes I wore on and off the stage, champagne by the magnum, handsome men to flirt and dance with. Paris was at my feet, *petite*, but there was no resisting Armand when he strode into my life. The type of man of whom I could expect few concessions. Here at El Kadia his tent was struck and, like Ruth, whither he went I had to follow.'

'You never regretted your decision, Nanette?' Roslyn asked, always deeply interested when her hostess talked of the past.

'One must never regret a deep love, no matter what

pains or sorrows it brings with it.' Nanette removed her spectacles and slid them into a velvet case. Then she came to sit beside Roslyn's curled-up figure on the cushioned daybed. The anchusa-blue eyes wandered over the girl.

'Three weeks with us and you begin to look less fragile. That is good!' She nodded, pleased. 'You feel better, my child? Less nervous of us, more settled in your mind?'

'I feel heaps better,' Roslyn assured this gracious woman who had been so kind to her. 'Your desert air is a wonderful tonic.'

'Tristan must take you out riding in the desert now you are no longer convalescent.' Nanette took hold of Roslyn's left hand and studied its slim bareness. Armand's ring no longer blazed on her third finger; she had locked it away in a drawer with the Juliet cap ... somehow they seemed to belong together.

'It hurt too much to go on wearing the ring?' Nanette murmured.

'It was rather loose on my finger and I was afraid of losing it.' Roslyn hesitated, then added: 'Nanette, would you let me return it to you? I was told it was yours – that you gave it to Armand when he became twenty-one.'

'Ah yes, a romantic conceit of mine that each of my grandsons give a ring I had loved to the girl of his choice. A ring blessed by love should be lucky – or so I thought.' The anchusa eyes dimmed with pain. 'No, the ring is now yours, *petite*. All that you have of Armand ... yet not all! There are things in the play-den used by him and Tristan when they were children. Diaries in which they wrote. Oddments they collected. Tristan must show you! It might help if you could touch those things, his books and boyish possessions. They might help you establish a link with him.'

Roslyn should have welcomed the suggestion, instead it made her feel cold. It was almost as though she were afraid of the lean, dark ghost who might haunt the play-den.

Each day Nanette inspected the house with the Arab boys to ensure that they were doing their work properly, and upon being left to her own resources Roslyn mounted the staircase that led to the harem tower. It had become a favourite retreat of hers. At any time she liked sitting up there among the tubbed flowers and bits and pieces of sun-faded furniture. The desert could be seen for miles, an expanse of amber that ran into combers like the sea; changing and beckoning, exciting her one minute, then giving her an illusion of peace the next.

The other day Jakoub had called it the Garden of Allah, when he had brought her a glass of orange juice and some of the star and crescent-shaped biscuits made from a harem recipe from the old days, when veiled girls had taken their leisure on the tower.

The Garden of Allah, Roslyn mused, as she sat in an old wickerwork chair and let her fingers play with some nearby flowers. Her shade hat was pulled well down over her eyes, for during the daylight hours you couldn't look directly at the sunburned sands without getting tears in your eyes. The vista was one of splendid savagery, rising in the distance into the burning peaks of the Gebel d'Oro, where Barbary brigands were said to have a stronghold.

It sounded too fantastic to be believable in this day and age, but like all legends and fables it appealed to the imagination. Peaks of petrified fire, where djinns and storm-gods had their abode ... would Tristan take her as far to see them? she wondered.

Then all at once she was leaning forward, her attention caught by an Arab on horseback, galloping like the wind across the sands, his dark cloak billowing into a wing that seemed about to lift rider and horse into the blue.

When they were gone, the desert seemed strangely empty. A silence after a paean of music, that was how it felt. Roslyn brooded under her shade hat in the silence, then she reached for the book she had brought with her and buried her nose in it until lunchtime.

Duane Hunter had turned up in his sudden fashion. It seemed he had something to discuss with Nanette, a wage dispute that might cause trouble at the packing sheds when the harvest was ready to be gathered.

'You have my authority to settle these things as you see fit,' Nanette said to him as they sat at lunch. 'You know what you are doing, Duane, when it comes to business. And I have a suspicion that your real reason for turning up like this was that you felt the need for some feminine company. Come, admit that I am right!'

He didn't admit anything, but there was a smile edging his mouth as he poured wine for his grandmother. 'What a trusting woman you are, Nanette,' he drawled. 'Aren't you afraid that I shall take over the business behind your back?'

'You are far too British for tricks of that kind,' she said tartly. She stared sideways at him, then added: 'Take a holiday, Duane. A day away from the plantation will not hurt you, or the trees. It would make a nice change for all four of you young people to go into the city to look at the shops, to sail on the lake, and dance in the evening at a club. How long is it since you danced, *mon brave*?'

'Can he dance?' Isabela laughed, a gleam of excitement in her eyes, Roslyn noticed. 'Duane, please agree to Nanette's suggestion. It sounds like fun.'

Isabela's red mouth held her plea like a kiss, and Roslyn saw Duane's brown skin tauten over the bones of his face; his eyes on those seducing lips were green as a wolf's.

'What of you, Tristan?' he drawled.

'I think the idea an excellent one.' Tristan was busy with his cold lamb in mint aspic.

'And what of our little girl lost?' Duane glanced at Roslyn.

She flushed and hated him, and wished she might see the city of El Kadia with Tristan alone. She half turned to Tristan, as though seeking his protection, and he looked up and flashed her a smile. 'Roslyn is coming, of course,' he said, and that settled the matter.

Luncheon grew gay, because the prospect of an outing had put Isabela in a sparkling mood. She talked about Portugal where she had danced and sung in the wine. 'I love to dance almost as much as I love to sing. You will dance with me, Duane. Promise!'

He looked at her, his expression enigmatic.

Isabela gazed back at him, too sure of her own beauty to doubt that she could replace with her substance the shadow of another woman. With a graceful, audacious gesture she plucked a red rose out of the bowl upon the table and threw it straight at him. He caught and crushed it in his hand, the scent of it sudden and strong in the air.

'Saturday will suit me best,' he said. 'We'll start early and go in the Renault wagon.'

'I have an idea,' Tristan was looking mischievous over the rim of his wine glass. 'Why do we not make a whole week-end of this outing? We could put up at a hotel and not have the bother of driving home in the dark. Besides, the girls will be tired.'

Duane looked as though that wouldn't have worried him in the least, but with a sudden lazy laugh he gave in to the idea, added that he couldn't stay for coffee and strode across the room to pick up something from one of the divans. A dark riding cloak, Roslyn saw. The kind an Arab would wear!

It was Duane whom she had seen on horseback from the harem tower, so at one with the desert, the sun and the fire-coloured mountains, that Isabela was going to have to use every artifice in order to lure him away from them.

Duane said *au 'voir*, and Roslyn watched him sweep

73

out of the room with Isabela at his side. She was smiling up at him, chattering away, vivid as a jay-bird beside a hawk.

'What has come over our Duane?' Nanette chuckled. 'Do you suppose, Tristan, that he can be falling in love?'

Tristan shrugged and handed Roslyn a peeled orange. 'As the Arabs say, *grand'mère*, a pretty woman is a snare into which the most wary of men is likely to fall.'

CHAPTER SIX

Roslyn admitted to herself that a week-end trip into the desert city of El Kadia would be interesting. She looked forward to a roam through the *souks*, and at this time of the year flamingoes were said to be seen on certain parts of the Temcina Lake.

It was Friday evening. Friends of Nanette's had come to Dar al Amra to dine and play cards, and Roslyn had slipped away now dinner was over to the seclusion of the harem tower. Her amnesia had been a topic of conversation at dinner, and talking about her loss of memory had left her feeling despondent.

Other people might find it intriguing to meet someone devoid of personal memories, but to Roslyn it was still frightening to have half her mind lost in a fog that just wouldn't lift. Sometimes she seemed almost to glimpse a ghostly outline, that stole into view out of the mist and then vanished again before the details of the place or the person became clear enough to be recognized.

It was maddening, bringing her close to tears, for she knew that one clear recollection would banish the fog and she would be a whole person again instead of – as Duane Hunter ironically put it – a little girl lost.

She wandered restlessly about the tower, the smoky chiffon of her dress giving an illusion of the veils worn by the girls of the harem. A moon had started, an Eastern crescent of fine silver, scattering stars from the tilting end of it. The night was warm and the palm fronds hardly stirred.

Space, and more space, Roslyn thought, gazing across the desert that created a peaceful forgetfulness that was not tortured like that of her amnesia. The desert was a garden of mystery, where moon-made shadows and low sounds drifted and died.

Then she grew still, unmoving and enchanted as there stole across the tower the haunting strains of *Il pleut dans mon coeur*, played on the guitar.

The music died away and she turned to face Tristan as he came to join her at the parapet, his guitar on a band across his shoulder. He was dark, tall and chivalrous as the troubadours of medieval Brittany, from whence the Gerards had sprung long ago. He had discarded his evening jacket and wore over his white shirt a jerkin of kidskin. She smiled warmly, thinking how different he was from his cousin, soothing and yet also gay, with eyes dark as blaeberries.

'I loved that song,' she said. 'It suited my mood.'

'Are there tears in your heart, Roslyn?' He lounged beside her, the moonlight gleaming on his dark head. '*Naturellement!* How could it be otherwise for you? Love doesn't die as easily as people, and I saw at dinner that our talk was upsetting you.'

'I feel so lost, Tristan,' she admitted. 'Sometimes I go groping after memory in such a panic, for I have to know about yesterday before I can be sure about tomorrow. You do see that?'

'Of course,' he gave an understanding nod. 'But it will do no good for you to worry. Your mind has etched indelible impressions of people, places and events in the past. At the moment they are obscured and naturally this is very troubling, but be sure they are there and one day they will suddenly emerge and you will know where you have been and where you are going.'

'You're very reassuring,' she said, with a little sigh that was like that of a comforted child. 'Play some more music, Tristan.'

'I don't know whether I should.' He was studying her face, a pale triangle, neither pretty nor plain but with

76

something pixieish about it. 'The guitar is the instrument of nostalgia and I don't want to send you to bed in a sad mood. Early tomorrow we are off on our week-end jaunt. You look forward to it, Roslyn?'

'Very much,' she said. 'I don't think I've ever been into an Eastern market.'

'The bazaars are fascinating, warrens of oriental craft and graft. I will introduce you to mocha coffee, and take you to the top of a minaret.'

'Sounds exciting.' She gave a little shiver of anticipation. 'Do you – do you suppose your cousin minded that I am going?'

'Why should he mind?'

'He – doesn't like me.' She fingered the rough stone of the crenellation where she stood; large emerald fireflies shone like gems in the milky dark. 'I believe he thinks me a fraud.'

'You?' Tristan smiled and touched her cheek, briefly. 'You would not know how to begin a deception, let alone carry one through. No, there is an abrasive quality in Duane and anyone sensitive is bound to be hurt by him. He is not a bad fellow, when you get to know him. A rough diamond out of the jungle.'

'No, a jaguar,' she said. 'He got wounded once, and now he takes no more chances on whether a friend or a foe confronts him.'

Tristan smiled in his wry, attractive way. 'Perhaps so. Like lightning, love is not always lethal, but sometimes when it strikes it leaves its mark for many years.'

Roslyn studied her companion as he brought his guitar round in front of him and begun to strum softly the love theme from his new opera. Haunting, holding a plea that grew gradually fierce until all tenderness seemed about to be lost, but wasn't quite lost as the final chords died away.

'It's lovely, and barbaric,' Roslyn said. 'It caresses and bruises.'

'Like love, of course.' His Gallic eyes smiled down at her. 'Love is subtle, a weapon and a web. Love is the madness that keeps men sane, though the emotion to a man is not quite the same as it is to a woman. A woman is bewildered if a man has several facets to his personality; a man on the other hand is charmed by a chameleon, a changing creature, a mistress, mother, counsellor and courtesan.' Tristan turned his dark gaze to the desert. 'You are easy to talk to, Roslyn, and also dangerous. Those grey eyes of yours draw out of a man the thoughts he usually keeps to himself.'

'I suppose I'm just a good listener,' she smiled. 'Anyway, what you have to say is always interesting.'

'Roslyn,' his hands touched her shoulders, 'you are a kind child, and I am sorry life had to hurt you so soon.'

She gazed up at him. They were within kissing distance, a girl and a man lost in a different way to each other, seeking the way home and driven in their search towards a passing haven. Tristan's lips found hers and he was holding her in his arms when high heels sounded on stone, and they broke apart to find Isabela looking at them.

The silver dipper of a moon poured its light on to her lovely face and Roslyn saw the scorn in her eyes. She had no use for Tristan's kisses, but he wasn't supposed to give them to another girl!

'Well, Isabela?' Tristan's arm stayed firm around Roslyn's waist.

'I thought it would be cool up here after that warm *salon* filled with cigarette smoke,' Isabela flicked a look of disdain over Roslyn. 'Evidently it is even warmer up here.'

Roslyn's cheeks were burning, yet there had been no passion in Tristan's kiss. What first kiss holds passion? It is a question seeking an answer, and Isabela had interrupted before that answer had been established.

Indian file, the three of them crossed the tower and

went down the stairs. In the corridor Roslyn said good night and hastened towards the vermilion door of her room. Inside the room she didn't switch on the light but stood with her back to the door, listening to her heartbeats and trying to recall her own emotions during the course of that kiss. Had she responded to it because Tristan resembled his brother Armand? Had she needed comfort, and men have only the one way of giving it?

She sighed, and wished Isabela had not been their witness.

Saturday morning dawned, and the air felt like wine when Roslyn went out into the Court of the Veils after breakfast. Duane was due any minute, but she had to take leave of Nanette and she flew on sandalled feet across the hall and up the stairs.

It was Nanette's custom these days to take breakfast in bed, and she was buttering a triangle of toast when Roslyn entered her room. The blue voile of her bed-netting was drawn back, framing her snow-blue hair, and her fine-boned face showed its age in the early morning light. She studied Roslyn unsmilingly, as she came and perched on the bedside, slim as a boy in a raspberry-red shirt and cream-coloured pants.

'You look gay as an urchin this morning, my child, so I take it you are now prepared to enjoy this week-end away from Dar al Amra. Tell me,' Nanette busied herself with the coffee pot, 'has my grandson anything to do with this change of heart?'

'Do you mean Tristan?' Colour came and went in Roslyn's cheeks; she guessed at once that Isabela had been in and planted a little mischief in Nanette's ear. 'That girl,' Roslyn could almost hear her, 'she appears to have forgotten Armand already. I saw her last night, kissing Tristan on the harem tower.'

'The Sleeping Beauty is a charming story, but this is

79

life, reality,' Nanette spoke gently but seriously. 'If you are seeking Armand through Tristan, who resembles him, you could both be hurt. I hope you realize that not all men take their kissing lightly.'

Roslyn glanced down at the clenched hands in her lap, and wished it were possible to hide all alone with the wounds other people seemed to want to tear open all the time. 'I wouldn't use Tristan for a probe,' she said a little sadly. 'He's far too nice for that sort of treatment – anyway, I'm just a child to him.'

Roslyn raised her rain-clear eyes. 'He kissed me because he feels sorry for me, he said so. And I let him kiss me because sometimes I feel a little sorry for myself.'

'I did not mean to upset you, *petite*.' A thin, veined hand closed over Roslyn's. 'It is that I have a concern for my young. I fuss in case life should bruise them, though I know full well that life is all the richer for the knocks we suffer and survive.'

The elderly woman and the young one faced each other for a long moment, then Nannette said briskly: 'Go to my toilet table, child, and fetch me that circular box. I have something in it which you might like, a trifle of no more use to an old woman.'

The trinket box stood on tiny feet, and Nanette delved into it and brought to light a bracelet set with panels that represented scenes from French fables. 'I was given this when I was about sixteen, and now I should like you to have it. It is winsome, no?' Nanette smiled and clipped the bracelet about Roslyn's wrist.

'It's charming, Nanette,' colour had run back into Roslyn's cheeks, 'but I don't know that I ought to let you give it to me.'

'It is given,' Nanette said with decision. 'It never appealed to my daughter, whose *mondaine* tastes, surprisingly, were not proof against the rugged looks and charm of the British planter whom she married. I saw them marry with trepidation, but thank heaven the marriage was a success. They soon had a child, Duane, and I knew that he would keep the gay, lively mind and body of my Celeste fully occupied. It would, you understand, *petite*, have been hard to bear had I thought her unhappy all those miles from me. She was much younger than my sons, the girl child my husband had always wanted, so her happiness meant all that much more to me.'

Nanette's eyes brooded on Roslyn's face, as though the wide eyes and youthful features reminded her a little of her daughter's, before she had married and gone away.

'Thank you for the bracelet, Nanette.' Roslyn leant forward and kissed the fine, pampered skin that stretched like silk over the beautiful bones of Nanette's face. 'I shall treasure it always.'

'Treasure what?' said a voice, and in through the door strode Duane Hunter, who had evidently come to collect in person the member who was holding up the expedition into El Kadia. Roslyn realized now that she had heard the car horn being sounded, but she had been absorbed in Nanette's confidences about Celeste.

She tensed, for a pair of tawny-green eyes were fixed on the bracelet her fingers leapt to cover. What inadequate cover! The enamelled panels glinted between the slimness of her fingers.

'I have just given Roslyn a keepsake,' his grandmother informed him. 'Well, it makes a nice change, Duane, to see you in civilized clothing. Enjoy this week-end. Relax, and forget the plantation.'

'I may do just that.' He grinned and bent over his grandmother, landing a kiss where Roslyn's lips had shyly rested. Roslyn hovered by the door. She wanted to dash away down to the car, but that would look childish. So she waited, smiled a nervous good-bye at Nanette, and preceded out of the door the tall figure in tropical tussore, a tawny silk shirt thrown open at the throat that was several shades tawnier.

They were half-way along the corridor when he caught at her left wrist and took a long, hard look at the panelled bracelet. She didn't look at him, but there was a glint of undersilver through her dark lashes as she felt the savage aliveness of his fingers. It was frightening that a man could be so alive, filled with the kind of power that left a woman with only her wit to defend her.

'Pretty,' he murmured. 'The bracelet, I mean.'

'I know what you mean.' Her chin tilted. 'You said I was after perquisites, didn't you, Mr. Hunter?'

He stared down at her with narrowed eyes, then she gave a gasp as his grip tightened and she was brought up against him, her imprisoned hand an inch from his face. 'No one could be as innocent as you look,' he crisped. 'Only a fool, or a child, and you're neither.'

'Let me go!' She struggled for release, wildly, helpless as a bird caught by a cat. 'You're never happy unless you're picking on me! I – I suppose you'd like me to drop out of this week-end trip, but I'm not going to – just to please you.'

'I want you doing nothing to please me, Miss Brant.' He gave a derisive laugh. 'Whether or not you come on this trip makes no difference to me. Why should it? You're not my type.'

'You're not mine, either,' she blazed back. 'You're arrogant, insulting, and just about the easiest man to hate that I've ever met!'

'Have you met plenty, besides Armand?' he drawled.

'I – don't know.' Her wrist was hurting from trying to drag it free of his grip. 'I could be anything, all the things you say, but there is one thing for sure. The aversion is mutual, Duane Hunter. I hate you touching me and coming anywhere near me and I pity any woman who thinks you worth loving. You seem to think you're the only human being who ever got hurt or disillusioned. Lots of people love someone and end up without them through one cause or another, but I hope they don't all get like you. Hard and bitter, and without charity. Charity may be a cold word to some, but I'm grateful to Nanette for offering hers to me. It comes straight from her heart, and I'd sooner be struck down than play Judas to so kind and generous a person.'

Roslyn tossed back her head and a finger of sunlight poked through a window and stroked the fair, cropped hair above her jade-grey eyes. Her cheeks and her throat were hollowed, holding shadow. Her skin was pale, but her lips seemed aflame from the words that came out of them.

'Nanette knows about love as I don't think you do, Mr. Hunter. How frail we are in love, yet how strong. How blessed if we don't let the petty things destroy the great; how cursed if we let them destroy the beauty. I have no memory at the moment, and that is the truth, but I want to remember. I want to know what it felt like to have love, even if I have now lost it.'

In the silence, held close to him as she was, she felt the beating of his heart. Such intimacy was unbearable, and when the horn of the Renault suddenly blared, shattering the silence, she tore free of him and ran – down the stairs, across the hall, out into the courtyard and the sunshine where Tristan stood awaiting her.

He smiled and held out a hand to her. Isabela was already in the wagon, up front, powdering her nose and looking proud and distant as Queen Nefertiti. Roslyn slid along the roomy back seat of the wagon and watched as Duane took his place in front of the driving wheel. Doors slammed. Tristan was installed beside herself, Isabela was casting a glance at Duane's brown profile as he started the Renault and the shadow of the horseshoe arch was over them, then the green and gold shadows of the plantation as they sped along the car track.

Once out of the plantation, the sun was brazen over the

desert, and in a while they passed an encampment of black tents pitched about a water-hole. There were camels chewing harsh-looking thorn as though it was the softest grass, and a herd of mixed sheep and goats. Women clustered with jars about the water-hole, their dark Bedouin faces uncovered. A robed man butchered meat near one of the long, low, hair tents, and there hung over the scene a Biblical quality, unchanged down the centuries.

Mary and Joseph might have passed such an encampment on their journey, Roslyn thought, and been given hospitality by people who looked exactly like those.

Isabela remarked that real Arabs were certainly not like the sheiks in novels and films.

'I should hope not!' Duane said. 'Those are real men, and women, hewn out of the fire and ice of their land. In actual fact, a desert sheik is little more than a shepherd, a nomad wanderer who opens his eyes for the first time in a hair tent, who marries a girl of his own tribe and rarely takes a second wife, let alone a third or a fourth. The sky is his roof, the sand his floor, his bed, and finally his last resting place.'

'You talk about the men of the desert as though you envy them, Duane.' Isabela's laugh was a low, mocking peal. 'Don't tell me that such a life would appeal to you?'

'Of course it would appeal to him,' Tristan broke in, winking at Roslyn. 'Duane has a very primitive disposition, have you not, *mon ami*?'

'Sure,' there was a hint of a smile in Duane's voice. 'I mixed with forest Indians right from a boy and learned from them how to trap fish, track game, and ride the wild waters in a native skiff. It was quite a life ... while it lasted.'

'Any regrets about leaving?' Tristan was getting out cigarettes. Roslyn shook her head, but Isabela – who did not smoke on account of her voice – took one for Duane, lit it between her ruby lips and put it between his. A

84

plume of smoke wafted over his shoulder, mingling with the smoke Tristan was making.

'Sometimes I get a yen to smell again the smoky balls of wild rubber,' Duane admitted. 'To sink my teeth in a fat papaya and eat fish cooked in wild banana leaves. In one section of the plantation out there we grew tonka beans – God, the perfume of them! There were pacas to hunt, spider-quiet. And caymen. Tail of alligator is quite a dish.'

'Duane, really!' Isabela was looking disgusted.

'It's true, my dear.' The drawl was back in his voice. 'The jungle is the Devil's Paradise and I was well at home in it. I revelled in the roar of rain like a waterfall, the thud of pagan feast drums, and the way the setting sun turned the rivers to wine. *"Llora, llora, corozón,"* sang the Indians.'

'And what are the charming words supposed to mean?' Isabela asked.

' "Weep, weep, my heart." ' Sitting behind them Roslyn saw their eyes meet and hold, then his cynical smile cleaved the copper of his cheek. 'Doesn't make a lot of sense, does it, the things we get to care about? Those rain forests were hot as hell more often than not, yet there were times when they thrilled like an angel's kiss.'

Roslyn couldn't help staring at those two in front of her, even though it was like peeping in through a window at two people who were kissing. Isabela's kiss would not be angelic, surely? She was a spoiled and tempestuous beauty, the sort to demand of the man she married *her* way of life. Those two would certainly have to learn to compromise, Roslyn thought, if the alchemy between them was growing into love.

'Did you witness any pagan rites during your years in the bush?' Tristan inquired of his cousin.

'Several,' Duane threw over his shoulder. 'Plenty of witchcraft flourishes in the jungle, and it's easy enough to believe in rain gods and fire spirits when the *mae da lua*

85

cries weirdly from the treetops at nightfall and the river holds the moon. How she shakes, Jaci the Moon Goddess possessed at the height of her beauty by the Devil River.'

'Sounds fascinating,' Tristan murmured. 'Duane, I cannot remember you talking about all this before.'

'Perhaps I had to be in the right mood,' Duane shrugged.

'A relaxed mood, *minho cara*,' Isabela purred. 'Does it not feel good to be unchained from your galley-bench?'

He gave a laugh, then stretched his hand to the map-compartment and took something out of it. Isabela gave a small gasp, then Duane tossed the object over his shoulder, presumably for Tristan to catch, but it landed in Roslyn's lap.

A shrunken head the size of a black-brown orange, lank hair hanging about the sealed eyelids, the lips sewn into a grimace. Tristan took hold of it by the hair and held it aloft.

'*Mon dieu!*' he exclaimed. 'Is it real?'

'The genuine thing.' Duane glanced round with a quick grin, his eyes on Roslyn. He added for her benefit alone: 'That's what I'd have looked like, had the Jivaro taken my head for a *tsanta*.'

'Why do they do it, Duane?' Tristan asked. 'Do they still take heads and shrink them?'

'Occasionally,' Duane replied. 'It's done to satisfy family or tribal honour, and each man who takes a head must, in due course, have his taken by revenging members of the beheaded one's family. So it goes on, like blood feuds out here in the desert, and vendettas in places like Corsica and Sicily. We all know these practices are dying out, but they aren't quite dead.'

'Do they ever take female heads?' Isabela voiced a question which Roslyn was dying to ask.

'No, women are safe in that respect,' he chuckled. 'Actually, Indian women don't lead a bad sort of life,

86

that is if they steer clear of male magic when it's practised. The *moko-moko* caught near an all-male gathering, especially with the chiefs and medicine-men present, is asking for trouble. Apart from that, they are courted and loved in a way a lot of civilized women might envy. What young bachelor in our society would submit to being bound in a sack of fire-ants in order to test his endurance for the state of marriage?'

'*Nom d'un chien*, but that sounds a bit drastic,' Tristan laughed. 'Were I an Indian, I would remain a bachelor.'

'What if you were madly in love, *mon ami*?' Isabela turned round and fixed a pair of brilliantly curious eyes on Tristan's face. 'Is not love worth some suffering?'

'I really wonder about that,' he replied. 'It seems to me that in our society suffering has little value, and that a careless regard for the feelings of others is far more rewarded. In short, the sensitive people, who are more capable of all the better feelings, including love, are the ones who receive less and deserve more. No wonder they are now girding themselves in the armour of ambition. Who can blame them? They are being forced into it in order to survive in a so-called civilized world.'

'Tristan,' Isabela opened wide her eyes, and her smile was mock-hurt, 'what a lecture! Is it for me alone, or is Duane included?'

Tristan's eyes dwelt on his cousin's bronze head, then he smiled in his wry, Gallic way and handed Isabela the *tasanta*. In a way it was a significant gesture. The head to you, it seemed to say; the heart you may yet have to win.

Roslyn glanced out of the window beside her and saw that they were leaving the sand-seas behind them. They rolled away, lost suddenly under the immense arch of the Bab el Kadia, the gate of the city, set in sun-scaled walls that stretched right and left like the huge ramparts of a fortress community.

CHAPTER SEVEN

THEIR Arab hotel was rather like an old castle to look at. It was picturesque, but there was no running water and it had to be brought to their rooms in earthenware jars.

Roslyn liked the hotel right away, for it was near the Temcina Lake, precariously perched on cliffs that tumbled in heaps and mounds to the shore. She could see the lake from the balcony of her room, a glittering expanse of cool water with an island set in the middle of it like a green gem. Roslyn stood drowning in the sight. She felt a longing to plunge into the water, and knew that she must be able to swim.

She closed her eyes and fought to recapture the tangible sensation of cleaving water ... moonlit water, stars in it, and someone running along a shore holding out a hand to her. Roslyn put out her own hand, but met only emptiness. Her eyes flew open, and her dazed glance fell to the courtyard below.

Duane Hunter stood with legs wide-planted beneath her balcony, his jacket discarded, the sun biting into his throat and arms.

He was studying her with curious eyes ... Juliet on her balcony, holding out a supplicating hand. Colour rushed into her cheeks, and she turned into her room, where she stood for long moments with her hands pressed to her temples, wrenching at the closed door in her mind ... the door that had opened a fraction and then closed again. She had half-remembered something – and it was connected with a lake!

She had a wash, then joined the others downstairs. Her heart was pounding, her cheeks were faintly flushed with excitement. That night when the others were in their rooms, safely asleep, she intended to go down to the lake-shore. There would be a moon so she would be able to find her way down the cliffs. Alone by the water, moon-dappled, she might come to grips with that elusive figure, running towards her with outstretched hand.

'I think all four of us need to wet our throats before we go into town,' Duane said, and a waiter brought cool drinks to them at a table under the lime-flowers of the patio.

Near where they sat the crumbling castle walls merged with the cliffs and a pair of black-tailed storks had made a home there, a scruffy flat nest on which they lounged without taking any notice of the human beings who sat only a few feet away from them.

'They aren't a bit nervous,' Roslyn said, intrigued.

'The stork knows he's a sacred bird in the East,' Tristan told her. 'A slayer of serpents, a bringer of good luck to the house on which he builds his nest.'

'If a stork lodged on my roof,' Isabela murmured wickedly, 'I should fear he was bringing me a little bundle.'

Duane chuckled, then he said: 'I thought Latin women liked *pequiños*. They seem to have pretty large families.'

'Children are cute,' she shrugged, 'but I have my career. Also the old-fashioned notion that women belong only in the home is no longer acceptable to Latin women of pro-gressive ideas. Duane, surely you are not in favour of women being tied down to domesticity?'

'Nothing animate should be tied down,' he agreed, 'but most men like the idea of perpetuation and having offspring is about the best way of achieving it.'

'What a cold-blooded thing to say!' The words broke from Roslyn before she could stop them. 'Children are for loving and laughing with. They aren't just mirrors for a man to see himself reflected in. Is that all yours will ever mean to you, Mr. Hunter?'

Duane quizzed her over the rim of the glass in his hand, then his teeth snapped whitely in an unkind laugh. 'I am not a sentimental man, Miss Brant. I learned quite young to look facts in the face, and the idea that love and marriage are worth getting romantic about is strictly – for the birds.' He gestured at the storks on their nest, their sun-coloured bills touching as they snoozed.

Roslyn looked away from him, out across the lake, scornful of herself for letting him ruffle her up. How, she wondered, could any woman want a man so bereft of tenderness? He had deliberately mangled it in himself . . . if it had ever existed!

'Is it really necessary for us to get dusty and hot down in those noisome *souks*?' Isabela leaned back in her chair, a curved figure in white, cinnamon-patterned silk, the lobes of her ears covered by cinnamon-stones. She yawned delicately behind her hand. 'I think it would be a bore.'

'Roslyn wishes to see the *souk*s,' Tristan flicked a glance over Isabela. 'You will grow fat, you know, if you laze about all the time!.'

'Fat?' The enormity of the idea! 'How dare you?'

He had dared, his dark Latin eyes full of mischief as Isabela jumped to her feet and snatched up her wide-brimmed hat. 'Well, come along all of you,' she said, and the glance she gave Roslyn was one of open dislike. Roslyn caught it, but hardly cared. You couldn't be liked by everyone, and being liked by Tristan made up amply for the animosity of the other two.

They went ahead down the pavement of wide, uneven steps; Roslyn and Tristan were content to follow, enjoying the glimpses of peacock-water, sails and palms through oriental arches. The others were now out of sight, lost in the narrow streets of high-walled houses that led into the heart of the bazaar district.

The streets looped, noise-filled lanes that led into each other and out again, where it would be as easy as anything for a stranger to lose herself.

The *souks* of the East, covered by trellises that cast tawny-dark stripes over robes and faces and merchandise. Baskets of flowers lined a narrow stairway. Mimosa, carnations, roses and lilies – bride of flowers – to bloom gaily until the heart wilted them in a matter of hours. On grass panniers, like great shields, there were oranges and pumpkins, golden melons, and pomegranates, some of them sliced like hearts to collect the dust that rose under the shuffling *babouches* of the crowd.

Left and right there was something fascinating to take note of, like the bearded scribe to whom women dictated letters. A couple of women wore the mysterious *burkha* that left only slits for the eyes; sooty eyes with an Eastern charm to them.

'Don't you find those women intriguing?' Roslyn shot a smile at Tristan, close to her side in the crowd, the tips of his fingers touching hers. 'It must set a man wondering, to see only a pair of painted eyes and fingers dipped in henna.'

He returned her smile, and she thought again how attractive he was. 'You, *femme blonde,* I find far more intriguing,' he said. 'Do you know what the African sun has done to your hair?'

'Bleached it,' she said flippantly.

'*Mais non,*' he protested. 'Gilded it, and now you look like an Attic slave-boy. Quite charming, I assure you, with those pants.' His fingers took hers, sudden and hard. 'But tonight you will wear a dress and we will dance, no?'

She nodded, not looking at him, her heart beating quickly as she remembered the lake-shore assignation she had planned for herself.

Oh, the smells of this place, tingling in her nostrils. Green mint, overflowing from baskets. Crushed herbs and spices mingling. Henna in panniers, cosmetic of joy. Arab coffee to which vanilla had been added, goat meat on the spit, onions, warm bread; musk and amber as they passed a perfume seller.

Tristan wanted to stop and buy her a phial of some exotic scent, but she laughingly shook her head and said she wasn't the type. His eyes met hers, brushing down over her face to her lips. 'You child,' he said, and let her hurry him on to the silk-spinners' corner, where she fingered the citron and Meccan-green stuffs, and drew her fingers down a length of night-soft velvet.

She just wanted to feel and be aware; to take into herself the hot, clamouring, aroma-rich fantasy of the souks.

Irresistible fantasy in the shape of a teller of fates; a vendor of love and hate potions, amulets to ward off sickness, to ensure the birth of a male child, or to lessen the dangers of a journey. When the old wizard held out in his palm a tiny gilded Hand of Fate, Roslyn knew she had to have it. She dug into her purse, shaking her head at Tristan. 'You can't buy good fortune for me,' she protested. 'I must pay for it.'

The little hand was quite perfect in detail, though not of any real value ... except as a charm. Roslyn fingered it as they wandered on. Would the little hand work the magic that would lead her out of the half-land in which she was lost?

She felt Tristan looking at her and summoned an airy smile for him.

'You must let me buy you a *hadya* of some sort,' he said. 'Come, what would you like? Beads, a scarf, or a scarab ring?'

'*Hadya*,' she murmured. 'It means gift, doesn't it? All right,' she pointed at something that had been wringing her heart ever since their entry into the *souks*. 'Buy me a cage of singing birds.'

'You strange child!' he exclaimed. 'What will you do with them?'

'Let them go.' She was regarding the caged birds with

a look of pain in her eyes. The tiny things sang because it was half dark in the *souks*, and Roslyn couldn't bear their desperate little songs.

Tristan strode over and bought one of the bigger cages in which nine or ten birds were imprisoned, and they walked on out of the noisy, trellised lanes into sudden sunlight that made Roslyn blink. She put on her hat and pulled the brim down over her eyes. Shaded now, and luminously grey, they met Tristan's. 'Thank you for my *hadya*,' she said. 'Now I'd like to go somewhere quiet and let the birds fly away.'

'I know the perfect place,' Tristan said, 'if your feet can stand some more walking? Prowling the *souks* can be hard on the feet and we have been in there rather a long time. Where, I wonder, could Isabela and Duane have got to?'

'Isabela wasn't keen on seeing the *souks*, so perhaps she persuaded your cousin to take her somewhere less crowded,' Roslyn said casually.

'Yes, they did appear to want to be by themselves.' Tristan smiled down at her, carrying without embarrassment the cage of birds so soon to be given their freedom. 'But we do not mind each other's company, do we? We will perform our errand of mercy, then find ourselves a cool café and have mocha coffee, just as I promised.'

'What about the minaret?' she asked. 'When shall I see that?'

'By starlight, *chérie*. We will put out our hands and touch the stars.'

'How exciting,' she smiled, a catch in her throat.

They climbed the staired streets side by side, passing the blank-walled Arab houses in which high, studded doors were set. Mysterious houses, their inner life never revealed to the stranger, though Roslyn knew from Nanette that Duane had Arab friends who made him welcome and shared with him their hunting falcons ... evidently the greatest of honours out here in the east.

She and Tristan climbed out of the town and came to an old ruin. Sand covered the broken columns and shifted through the courtways, and all that was left of the walls made nesting nooks for storks, the serpent slayers. All but one corner, where a coign of carved stone defied erosion, the remainder of what long ago had been a bastion. From beneath it the city of El Kadia looked like a huge buff-cream honeycomb, nibbled here and there, its minarets rising into the air like sticks of candy.

'This is the place I told you about, Roslyn – from now on known as the Bastion of Angelot.' He hoisted a leg upon some broken stonework and watched Roslyn open the cage and release the little birds into the honey-blue sky.

'I am not a little angel,' she grimaced as she smiled. 'Birds just weren't made to be caged – what shall we do with the thing?'

It was made from osier and not worth much, so he crushed it underfoot and kicked the remnants out of sight. 'There, as you hate cages so much.'

Roslyn faced him, silent for a moment, then a diffident smile touched her lips. 'Do you think me odd?' she asked. 'I know those birds might fly again into the nets that caught them before, but for a while they'll be free and happy.'

'Moments of happiness are all anyone can expect.' He looked wry and grave at the same time. 'When we face up to that, we can perhaps call ourselves grown up.'

'I shouldn't want to gorge on happiness all the time,' she said. 'I should be afraid of growing surfeited, blunted against joy in the feel and smell and texture of things. They are the real possessions of life, aren't they? If you are blind but aware, you are not blind.'

'Suffering has made you wise, *chérie*.' His hand was

gentle under her chin as he raised her face to him. 'But there is another kind of awareness, you know. The awareness of what is in one's heart and what to do about it.'

'I – know,' she said.

'I should like right now to finish the kiss we started last night, Roslyn, but I am not going to.'

'I understand, Tristan.' And there was no need to say more, for they could communicate without words. She didn't have to say that he looked like the pictures of Armand she had been shown, and that the arms she wanted around her might be another's. They didn't need words or embraces right now, only the mutual peace of standing beside the sun-warmed bastion, listening to the ghostly eddies of sand whispering about their feet.

'Come,' he said at last, 'let us go and have luncheon.'

Suddenly feeling as released as those little songbirds, Roslyn wanted to eat *à l'arabe*, and this they did at a small terrace-café shaded by the mushroom dome of a nearby mosque. They had *bourak*, a tasty roll made of minced mutton, sage and mint, and baked in a light pastry. Then *kus-kus* of semolina, rich with cream and studded with pieces of apricot, prunes and sweet almonds.

Over small glasses of mocha coffee, dark and rich, Tristan told her about Paris, the *cocotte* of cities, and his conflict in the beginning about attending the Academy of Music instead of learning the running of the plantation. 'My father was then alive, but already a sick man, and had it not been for Nanette, who understood so well my need to express myself in music, I should have supervised Dar al Amra without any of the passion that Duane gives to the place.'

'Is it passion that he feels?' Roslyn brooded on the arrogant, hawk-face of the man. 'I should have called it ambition.'

'Some of that, of course.' Tristan ran a finger round the rim of his coffee glass. 'Ambition for Dar al Amra to be first class, the most fertile of plantations, king of them all. I could never have felt like that, and how I blessed the turn of events that made it possible for him to come and take charge of things. In many ways he is a far more able man than I. I am a dreamer, Duane is a realist. I sometimes envy him for having both feet firmly planted on the ground, and yet I wonder what flight of ruined fancy makes him cling to the things of the earth and deny heaven.'

'A woman, perhaps.' Roslyn felt sure it had been.

'Yes, in most cases it is a woman.' Tristan glanced up with a smile, 'Do you like mocha coffee?'

'I've liked every moment of this morning, Tristan. The *souks*, and the songbirds you let me give back to the skies. Our lunch, talking about Paris and your music.'

The dome of the mosque cast its jade shadow over them, and they sat there as the streets emptied of people and the shutters closed above the red and blue Hands of Fate. Their waiter stood in the doorway of the café in a resigned attitude. Crazy Europeans, he seemed to be thinking, making talk when they could be taking siesta.

His *babouches* shifted restlessly.

'We cannot stay,' Tristan murmured. 'We have to shatter this perfect moment, or drive that poor fellow quite crazy.'

She watched the waiter come with an air of relief to their table, and she thought, with abrupt melancholy, that what was now shattered could never be replaced. Perfection couldn't be, and the next time of happiness waited to be carefully shaped, like a pot on the wheel, to emerge in loveliness, or with a flaw that made you careless of breaking it.

Roslyn opened her powder-compact and wiped some of the shine from her nose. As she dropped the compact back into her bag, the gleam of her tiny Hand of Fate caught her eye. The talisman she had bought in the *souks*,

96

all that was tangibly left of the happy hours that had sped so swiftly.

Sad, and also frightening, that what had been could never be quite the same again. You could never go back to see again quite the same look on a face, or hear again the same note in a voice. No lance of sunlight, no wedge of shadow was sculpted the same as before. Everything moved on and changed with every movement of the hand of time.

'If we went to the lake, there would not be a boat available at this hour,' Tristan said, as though reading in her eyes her reluctance to return to the hotel.

'It's hot,' she said. 'We had better go back.'

So they panted up the hill, the cabs deserted of drivers, the city as still as if under a spell. 'The city sleeps and only Beauty and the Prince are awake,' Tristan quipped, the perspiration making his hair cling in dark squiggles to his forehead.

Wearily they walked into the hotel and Tristan took their keys from off the wall behind the empty reception desk and they trudged upstairs to their rooms. Tristan unlocked her door for her.

'Have a rest. I want to take you out again tonight.' He leaned against the wall and his eyes flicked her boyish pants and shirt. 'I hope you brought a dance dress with you?'

She nodded, then had a thought. 'Supposing I can't dance?'

'Then I shall teach you.' His eyes creased in a half smile. 'I shall enjoy plucking the veils one by one from those wide grey eyes of yours — I think you have many things to learn.'

'Meaning I'm naïve?' Her cheeks grew pink and this added to her sunflushed look. 'You're a man of the world — it's a wonder I don't bore you.'

'You know you don't bore me.' His dark eyes followed

her blush. 'See, you are too young not to feel flattered that a man finds you appealing, and not old enough to be coy or calculating about it. Armand did grow up in Europe! I used to think he liked his girls to bubble and bounce.'

'Perhaps with Armand I did behave like that.' She shrugged. 'Who knows? I certainly don't, and we're all said to be split personalities.'

'The image is not always the truth, to be sure.' He smiled, took hold of her wrist and brushed his lips across her pulse. 'I will take a chance on your essential inability to bubble and bounce – I hope, Roslyn, that the dress is a pretty one—'

'What a charming scene,' drawled a voice. 'Tristan and Ysolde, I presume?'

A door had opened across the corridor and when Tristan turned sharply to look, Roslyn saw past him the figure of Isabela Fernao. There was something about her that sent a small thread of shock through Roslyn, then she realized that Isabela had on a flowered chiffon robe, the bedroom kind; a sleek nude leg showed beneath the long folds for an instant, and her luxuriant hair was loose on her shoulders.

The room out of which she had stepped was not hers. Behind her in the doorway stood Duane, his hair a coppery muzz above sardonic eyes, his shirt open like a jacket to the band of his slacks.

'Where have you two been all this time?' Isabela demanded. 'Did you get lost?'

· 'I think we did.' Tristan was still holding Roslyn's wrist, and she had a feeling he implied something subtle. 'And what became of you – and Duane?'

His eyes flashed to his cousin, tall behind Isabela in the doorway of *his* room, from out of which she had strolled in her bedroom robe.

'We went into the *mellah*,' Duane's voice was lazy as

the relaxed posture he had now assumed. 'Isabela wanted to buy a length of gaberdine – didn't you, honey? When we came out, we looked for you two, but you must have been deep in the heart of the bazaar. Still,' his gaze fell to the wrist Tristan held captive, 'I don't suppose either of you missed us.'

'And vice versa,' Tristan said smoothly.

'My dear,' Isabela was looking Roslyn up and down, 'have you had this poor girl out in the hot sun all this time? No wonder she looks such a wreck.'

'I – I must have a wash.' Roslyn backed into her room, adding with desperate humour: 'Tristan, my hand, please. It's the one I soap myself with.'

He let her go and, with a general *au 'voir*, she closed her door and retreated from what she believed was called a 'situation'. Poor Tristan! It must hurt when you saw exposed the clay feet of an idol, or more accurately the bare legs branching up into a golden torso equally bare beneath flowered chiffon.

Roslyn splashed her face, neck and arms with cool water. Her feet were covered with *souk* dirt and she gave them a good wash, then in her slip she lay on her Arab bed and watched the fan revolving in the paint-scaled ceiling. The air that was passed from blade to whirring blade was warm, but if she lay quite prone and didn't think too much about the heat it was bearable.

Later, when that brazen flame of a sun sank down, it would be deliciously cool. She strove to think of that, and that alone, but as she dozed she dreamed restlessly that she was back in the bazaar, and lost. Hopelessly lost. No one understood what she wanted and in the end she began to run, stumbling over giant pumpkins and getting entangled in yards of gauze that clung to her face like a veil. She came out into a square. The houses all round the square were blank-walled with slot windows like those in a castle . . .

She was very frightened. The walls seemed to be closing in on her, and she awoke, crying out in darkness. She sat up. Her heart was pounding ... there seemed no one, not a soul, who really understood how awful it was to be lost ... as she was.

She rose and put on the light. The room looked cheerless and felt airless; she had to get out of it. Throwing on her dressing-gown, she opened the balcony shutters and stepped outside to watch the last of the sunset.

Towards the west the sky was like an oriental tapestry that had run, carmine and dusky gold mingled with the palest green. A *muezzin* wailed from his minaret platform, then the tawny sky turned violet and the lake glistened duskily far below.

Her pulse beat fast under the hand she pressed to her throat. Later, she promised herself. When the moon is up; when everyone is asleep and I shall not be disturbed.

It was a little crazy, of course, and perhaps dangerous to go seeking ghosts in the moonlight, but nothing was going to stop her. She had to find out who it was who had run half-way out of the mists towards her ... down there on the lake-shore she felt certain that misty figure waited to materialize ...

But right now she must get dressed for dinner.

The dress she had brought with her was one of those she could not remember buying — a trousseau evening dress, knee-length, of knitted blue silk joined together over the shoulders like a herald's coat.

She looked like a page in it, she thought, studying her cap of fair hair and her mouth like a coloured bow against her sun-tinted skin that had a paleness underneath. A page carrying a secret in her eyes!

CHAPTER EIGHT

THEY assembled in the bare, stone-tiled lobby of the hotel, the two men in white sharkskin jackets over dark trousers; Roslyn in blue, her shoulders caped in the white fur which Nanette had insisted she borrow. 'It would be a little out of style in Paris,' she had said. 'But El Kadia is a city where past fashions mingle with the new – besides, it grows cool when the sun goes down.'

It did indeed, Roslyn thought, hugging the soft cape about her.

Ah, here came Isabela, making her glamorous progress down the stairs. She wore flame-coloured lace and long black gloves. Diamond bracelets flashed on the wrists of her gloves, and her cloak was of thick dark silk. With the gliding grace of the Latin she came across the lobby, her cloak billowing about the sheath of lace.

She shimmered flame-like as she stood poised in front of Duane, he the Lucifer who had ignited her to such fire and beauty.

'Have I kept you waiting?' Roslyn watched the upswing of her provocative glance. 'You must forgive me.'

'You look so fantastically beautiful,' he smiled, 'that tonight I might forgive you anything.'

'Would you forgive me for stealing your heart?' she asked softly.

'I might, if I had one to steal,' he said lazily.

'Don't pretend to be heartless.' Her face raised to his was like an exotic flower preening in the sun. 'You were not so – earlier on, were you, *mon amant*?'

He frowned slightly, Roslyn saw, and was about to speak, to say perhaps that she was making too public what should be kept private between them, when she turned gaily to face Tristan. 'Have you two men decided where you are taking us?' she asked. 'Of course, one cannot expect the kind of dance music and cabaret that one would enjoy in Lisbon – such a city! So gay and sophisticated, filled with theatres and night clubs.'

'Naturally El Kadia cannot expect to compete with Lisbon,' Tristan said dryly. He glanced at Duane. 'I thought we might go to the Dancing Fawn. What do you say, *mon ami*?'

'Sounds fine to me.' A quirk of a smile lifted the corner of Duane's mouth. 'You know more about the high life of El Kadia than I do, old man. I'm just a rugged planter, but I must say the name of the place stirs my interest. Do fawns dance?'

'Isabela dances,' she took his arm possessively, and as they walked out of the hotel ahead of Roslyn and Tristan it had to be admitted that they made a striking couple. The hunter with a gorgeous falcon on his wrist!

The spellbound city of that afternoon had a more mystic enchantment as the scimitar of a moon glided over the Eastern rooftops and turrets ... how could one doubt that even fawns could dance on such a night? The magic of it! Strange vibrations pulsed in the air, spicy fragrances thrilled Roslyn's nostrils, the old mysteries and intrigues still haunted this place, she was sure of it.

The enchantment she felt was in her eyes as she turned to enter the cab, making them jade-dark as she smiled at Tristan and slipped into the seat that held four people. Tristan followed, the door slammed and they shot away so quickly that Roslyn was thrown to the right against a crisp white jacket. Her startled eyes lifted only as far as the arrogant Hunter jaw ... she drew away hastily, electrified into a slim rod between the two cousins while Isabela sat at her ease by the window.

Their cab sped down the steep road she and Tristan had climbed in the sun, it zigzagged through narrow streets and with a loud blast of its horn joined the busy traffic of the central part of the city.

Roslyn looked out of the window beside Tristan and hoped the Dancing Fawn was not one of the bright, modern clubs whose lights had sprung to life along the main boulevard. Then her hopes soared again as they sped on past the shifting, neon-spangled crowds, among which a few women clung to the enticing veil but where in the main the dress was European and the faces bare to the gaze, many of them cosmopolitan. El Kadia was booming and expanding, and its citizens were discarding the old ways for the new ... what a pity, from a romantic point of view! The kaftan and the bournous had a style that nothing manufactured by modern tailors could hope to match.

The noise and the neons faded away, and Roslyn guessed happily that they were heading into the old part of the city. The realms of oriental fable, where the mysterious and the forbidden might still lurk behind the high walls and heavy oval-shaped doors.

The cab screeched to a halt in front of an archway, and Roslyn felt excited as she followed Tristan out on to the pavement. It was excitement, or high heels, that caused her to stumble as her brocade shoes encountered the cobbles. At once a pair of hands caught hold of her, saving her from a fall and crushing the soft fur that caped her shoulders ... Nanette's fur.

'Th-thank you,' she said, and without glancing round drew away from the touch. She had seen the green eyes flicking the white fur in the vestibule of the hotel ... another perquisite, that inspection had seemed to say.

She gave a slight shiver, and Tristan must have noticed as he took her arm. 'Are you feeling cold?' he asked.

'No, not in this fur cape.' Her voice lifted involuntarily. 'Your kind grandmother insisted that I borrow it.'

She sensed the half turning of a copper head and wondered, a trifle bleakly, why she bothered to defend herself. Her every action was suspect in Duane Hunter's eyes . . . it had been that way from the very beginning and she ought to be used to him by now.

Tristan was gazing down at her as they crossed the fore-court of the Dancing Fawn restaurant. 'You were so ready to enjoy this evening,' he murmured. 'What has upset you? Something has, I can tell by your eyes.'

She hesitated, but the words would not be held back. 'A feeling comes over me every now and again, Tristan, a kind of desperate, drowning sensation. I – I want to be pulled out of the darkness into the light, knowing myself. Knowing the other person I might be. Knowing what I've done and experienced . . . before the crash.'

'Of course, what else would it be?' His arm came round her in a sympathetic hug. 'It is easy enough for others, for me, to say don't worry, all will be well. All the same, my dear, would you prefer that we dine by our-selves? We can go somewhere else – shall we?'

Roslyn was tempted to say yes, but Duane would guess at once that she was running away from him. From his presence at a table for four. From his eyes across that table, watching as Tristan spoke to her, assessing the interest that his cousin was showing in her. He might even have the audacity to ask her to dance, knowing how much she hated him to touch her . . . and it would be a small satisfaction to be able to refuse him.

'No, let's stay,' she said. 'This place looks nice.'

Tristan ran his eyes over her upraised face. 'I think you will like it,' he said, and they entered the restaurant. There was a smell of saffron and smoke, the tinkle of indoor fountains, and a cloudy-amber lighting diffused from small table-lamps.

Couples were dancing to a small orchestra hidden in the shadows, and Roslyn caught a merging of flame lace and white tuxedo as they passed the dancers and sat down at their table for four. 'Shall we have a drink, or would you like to dance?' Tristan asked.

'I'd like a drink,' she said. 'Something daring.'

He beckoned a waiter and ordered a couple of daiquiris, his dark eyes resting on the blue simplicity of her dress as she slipped the white cape from her slim shoulders. 'You look rather lovely,' he said quietly. 'There is a flower that grows in the forests of France, it is blue and cool, but when plucked—' his hand moved as if to touch her, then drew back. 'Roslyn, you make me a little afraid of you.'

Music drifted over, people chatted and laughed around them.

'How could anyone be afraid of me?' she laughed nervously.

'Don't you know that men do fear women?' His smile grew quizzical. 'Especially those they are in danger of – liking too much.'

'Tristan,' her eyes grew wide with appeal, 'we mustn't talk about anything like that – I – I'm not ready—'

'I know,' he said quickly. 'We must wait until you are fully yourself again, with no longer a divided mind – or heart.'

The waiter brought their drinks, and large menus were placed on the table. Her daiquiri had a pleasant kick to it and she took small sips as she gazed round the restaurant. She liked the soft amber lighting which veiled the eyes without hiding their glimmer. Liked the subtle way in which East and West were blended, even in the dance music. A pair of dark hands thrummed the skin of a tambour. A *quembri* added its strange fluting notes.

'We will order our meal when Isabela and Duane come to the table.' Tristan was glancing through a menu. 'Are you hungry, Roslyn?'

She nodded, though in truth she felt too strung up to feel like eating. Then she tensed in her chair as the music died to a drumbeat and the dancers dispersed from the floor. She heard a woman's warm laughter, and then Isabela was at the table, looking pleased with herself as she slipped into the chair which Duane held for her.

Roslyn glanced up through her lashes, but as always that hawk-face of Duane's was quite unreadable. His green eyes flicked over her blue dress and the cool skin of her slim neck. Her fingers tightened on the glass holding her drink, and she wondered how Isabela could want a man who seemed to have no use for tenderness.

'You will both be amazed to hear that Duane is an excellent dancer.' She teased him with a smile as he sat down.

'Isabela seems to have assumed that my social activities were spent among the Indians, snake-dancing,' he said dryly. 'Shall we have champagne?'

He beckoned a waiter, while Isabela sat looking at him drowsily, behind long lashes. 'Where were your social activities spent?' she asked inquisitively.

'Some of them in Rio, my pet. Wicked Rio!'

'I see, Duane. You could not stand the monotony of the jungle all the time, eh? You needed the bright lights, and women in pretty clothes. Beware, *mon cher*, I shall worm out all your secrets one by one.' Her smile flashed across the table, assured as diamonds. 'The Dancing Fawn has quite a good orchestra, I must say, Tristan. You and the little Roslyn must try it.'

'We are going to eat first. Come, everyone, let us order dinner. The food here is as good as the music.'

The next few minutes were devoted to a study of the menus, and then the waiter arrived with their champagne. The cork sighed as it was withdrawn and a blue-blonde foam crowned the bottle. The bubbles were tiny, rising and popping in the glasses as the wine was poured. Tristan skimmed his nose across his brimming glass. 'Ah, I smell hawthorn, French soil and wood-violets,' he said, his lips in the wine.

'You have too much imagination,' Isabela scoffed. 'You see a Val de Loire label on the bottle and right away you are wafted to France. I wonder you don't buy a house there and settle down.'

'I shall, when I am ready,' he rejoined.

'And when will that be, I wonder?'

Roslyn felt the inquisitive flick of Isabela's eyes, and then to her relief the singer's attention was caught by something else. 'Duane, are those lotus blossoms?' She gestured to a cloak of flowers trained over the rim of a nearby fountain. 'Pluck one for me, please!'

'Are you going to eat it?' He laughed and did her bidding. 'They say that if you taste of the lotus you will never leave the land in which it grows.'

'Do you want me to put it to the test?' She teased his lips with the flower.

'I think you will find the *poulet braisé* on your plate much more to your taste,' he said mockingly.

'Brute!' She tucked the flower in her dark hair with Latin grace. 'I sometimes find it hard to believe that you are half French. Frenchmen have a respect for the romantic notions of women. They play along with our little games of make-believe.'

'I never did like games of make-believe.' His voice was suddenly a lash, low, stinging, causing Roslyn to look up from her plate before she could stop herself. Her eyes locked with his, and holding them he said to her, deliberately:

'Will you dance?'

She couldn't speak. Words were beyond her as he rose and came round to her, holding out a brown hand. 'Go on, Roslyn.' It was Tristan who spoke. 'You have Isabela's assurance that Duane will not march all over your feet.'

It was her feelings, not her feet, she was worried about,

and then Isabela said drawlingly: 'Does an amnesiac know whether she can do this or that? Roslyn might tread all over Duane's feet.'

'She's hardly likely to make much impression.' His hand closed round Roslyn's and with a slight but determined wrist-jerk he pulled her to her feet and led her from the table to the dance floor.

'I – I don't want to dance – *I can't!*' It was a desperate whisper, ending in a small gasp as with a sudden adroit movement he spun her into his arms and held her so there was no escaping him.

'Relax and enjoy the dance.' His downward glance was a cool stab of green. 'Armand was too fond of a gay time to have fallen for a girl who was not adept at most indoor sports.'

So that was what he was doing – *testing her*. A shudder ran through her and she stumbled over his feet, deaf to the rhythm of the music, blind to everything but the cruelty of this man. He made her stumble several times round the floor, then he let her go and, seething, she hurried ahead of him back to the table. Isabela sat there smiling. Tristan rose at Roslyn's approach, his straight brows cleft by a frown.

'Poor Duane!' Isabela rose also, her eyes agleam with malicious laughter as they swept from Roslyn's pale face to his. 'Let me make up for Roslyn's inadequacy, my dear.'

'By all means,' he said, and the next moment they were gone and Roslyn was left alone with Tristan. She sat down shakily, not looking at him as he reseated himself beside her. She took up her wine glass, but it shook in her fingers and she set it down again.

'That was a typical Byronic action of my cousin's!' Tristan lifted a hand and a waiter came to his side. He asked that their coffee be brought, with two Armagnac liqueurs.

Then he sat drumming his fingers on the table, frowning, abstracted, distant. Their coffee and liqueurs were soon brought to them, and Roslyn tipped the little glass of old-gold into her black coffee and drank it quickly, needing the false courage it would impart.

'Why Byronic?' she asked. 'Having been tortured he has to torture? I don't think that's the answer.'

'No?' Tristan studied her, his Gallic eyelids half drawn down. 'What is the answer?'

'He simply doesn't like me. He thinks I'm playing some sort of a game, and I – I begin to wonder—'

'What do you wonder?' Tristan leant towards her as she paused. She shook her head mutely, her every nerve hammering as the dance music died away and only seconds remained of her reprieve from Duane Hunter's presence.

'Shall we go?' Tristan asked, his eyes intent on her pale face.

She nodded, clutching at the white fur cape and pulling it around her, no longer too proud to run away.

The remainder of the evening was spoiled for her, though they climbed to the muezzin tower of a mosque like a narrow, decorative wedding-cake and she tried to reach for the stars that gleamed so close ... like ice flowers.

A breeze blew through the tower openings, and the moon was bruised by small clouds. 'I think I smell rain in the air,' Tristan said, and though he might not have been making an excuse to go, it sounded like one and her heart felt heavy as they made their way down the winding steps to the courtyard, where an attendant took the slippers they had had to put on upon entering the mosque.

The drive back to their clifftop hotel in a horse-drawn cab should have been a romantic one, but there was a feeling of constraint between them. They talked a little about the mosque they had just visited, and then he fell silent and seemed absorbed in his thoughts. She stole a look at his profile, and for the first and only time she saw a resemblance in him to Duane ... nose and chin hard-hewn, the gay good-humour of his eyes veiled behind brooding eyelids.

They arrived at the hotel and after the fiacre had driven away, they stood indecisive in the shadowy moon-light. 'Yes, I think it will rain before morning,' Tristan murmured, and then all at once he took her cold hands in his and gently crushed them. 'Stop tormenting your-self, *petite*. You have forgotten how to do certain things, and that is perfectly natural in the circumstances. People were able to tell you your name, your age, and other de-tails like that, but there are bound to be some things that you will have to learn to do again. Roslyn, are you listen-ing to me?'

'Yes, Tristan, of course.'

But why, ran her thoughts, did you look so distant and troubled at the Dancing Fawn? Were you doubting me?

'Suddenly you look as frail as a French egg,' he said with a gentle touch of humour. 'Tears not far away in those grey eyes. Come, let us go in. It is time you went to bed.'

As they mounted the stairs, having claimed their keys from behind the reception desk that seemed for ever deserted, a bubble of hysterical laughter began to rise in Roslyn's throat. 'Not a sound, not a cheep, everyone is fast asleep.' She chuckled. 'Do you suppose they are all enchanted? This place is rather like a castle, and we—'

'—are rather like the Sleeping Beauty and the Prince.' He stood looking down at her as they reached the door of her room, then he stroked with his long fingers the fur of her cape. 'If I kissed you, I wonder if it would break the spell that binds you?'

'No – we decided up at Angelot's Bastion that kisses might be dangerous.' The laughter died out of her eyes.

'They might make me forget that I have to remember your brother.'

At once, in the dim lighting of the corridor, she saw his warm expression replaced by coolness. He drew his hand away from her and with abrupt formality he wished her good night.

'Good night, Tristan,' she said, and determinedly closed her door between them.

It was eleven-thirty. Roslyn wandered restlessly about her room, waiting for midnight, when she would make her way down to the lake. Alone there, beside the whisper of water, she might find herself again.

She was still wearing her blue dress. It would be a pity to spoil it, clambering down that rocky cliff-path, and she took off her finery and replaced it with a pair of trews, a shirt and sandals. She hung up the blue dress, which Tristan had admired. Dear Tristan ... a perfect gentle knight. If Armand had been like him in ways as well as looks, then surely she must have cared for him?

She paced about her room, feeling on edge and troubled. You are Roslyn, they had told her at the hospital, and how could it be denied when she had been found clutching in her hand Armand Gerard's token of love?

How had she come by the ring, with its French inscription, if Armand had not given it to her?

And then she stood very still in that strange Arab room, her heart beat heavily as she seemed to hear a voice saying tauntingly: 'Good evening – Juliet.'

Her eyes darted round the empty room, taking in the blank walls that were symbolic of her unyielding blankness of mind. Suddenly, uncaring that Isabela and Duane were not yet back and settled down in their rooms, Roslyn hurried to her door, clicked off the light and stole out into the corridor. All was quiet and she carefully closed her door behind her and sped on rope-soled sandals to the stairs. . . .

There she was brought up short as the sound of voices floated upwards. They drew nearer, and Roslyn quickly darted across the corridor into the lavatory . . . then as the couple passed by the door, she heard the man say plainly: 'Deceiving people isn't a game I happen to want to be part of.'

'Don't be so stuffy,' the woman scoffed. 'You act as though it were a crime for a woman to enjoy a little make-believe.'

'Dishonesty is a crime, in my book,' he rejoined curtly. 'I know what a woman's lies can lead to, Isabela. What they can do to a man . . .'

'Poor Duane,' Isabela cooed, 'are you not going to allow another girl to mend that broken heart of yours?'

He didn't answer, and a few minutes later there came the sound of a door closing none too gently.

Roslyn had been holding her breath as she listened, now she released it and let herself out of the lavatory. She sped down the stairs and out of the hotel, and was breathing rapidly when she reached the cliff-path to the shore. The path was steep, rockier than she had realized, and she bruised her ankles as she started to climb downwards.

She had gone about half-way down when she paused for breath. Above her on the cliffs the hotel showed only one or two lights . . . it loomed like a black castle in the shifting moonlight, and looking back she realized that she had fled from it as though from a place of demons.

She commenced again her downward scramble, and reached at last the stones and sand of the shore. Tall palm trees stood here and there like sentinels, their slender trunks inclining towards the water of the lake, pooled with moon-mercury and cloud shadows.

Roslyn thrust her hands into her pockets and walked

along the edge of the lake. The night all around held the hidden chirr of cicadas, the rustling of palm-fronds and whirring of bat-wings. She wasn't nervous of these sounds, for they were all part of her mood. In a while she sat down on the sand and with her arms laced about her updrawn knees she gazed at the moonlit lake.

She didn't feel cold, or very aware of her surroundings. She was quietly, forcibly willing her mind to yield again as it had that morning.

The moon shimmered on the surface of the lake and made silver tracks . . . and suddenly a shiver of recollection ran through Roslyn. It was always fun swimming along the moon-trails, ever ready to duck out of sight because of the keeper who was always on the watch at night for poachers. The lake where they swam was near the airfield, and privately owned. They were not supposed to go there.

It was a big lake surrounded by alders, and willows that dripped catkins into the water. They used to dry themselves under the trees, and dress to the sound of their own low-pitched laughter and the hoot of the owls.

'Hush, we'll be heard,' Roslyn could remember saying, quite clearly. But her companion only laughed and performed a dance around the trees.

'Don't be scared of the keeper – he never comes to this end of the lake because he thinks we're wood-nymphs.'

Gay words, rippling back into Roslyn's mind as the water of the lake rippled.

Roslyn jumped to her feet, poised on the bank of the Temcina Lake, hearing again the laughter that was happy as a bell, silvery as the moon-trails on the water . . . *silvery as the other girl's hair.*

'What are you doing here?' a voice rapped out behind Roslyn . . . real, this time, not that of a ghost.

She swung round, her eyes wide with alarm as they

took in the tall figure behind her. *'You!'* she whispered, and then she turned and fled away along the shore, and as she fled, thunder growled over the lake.

CHAPTER NINE

THE moonlight played over the scene. A girl pursued in the age-old way by a man, but not in fun, in fear that made her cry out as he caught her where some palm trees interlaced, forming a trap into which she had run blindly.

He pinned her to the scaly trunk of one of the trees, easily, ruthlessly. 'You little wildcat!' he growled. 'Why did you run away from me? You might guess I'd chase after you ... don't you realize that a storm is brewing? Can't you hear the thunder?'

She heard only the thunder of her heart ... agitated by that wild chase along the shore and the closeness of this man, his black-sweatered chest against hers, her limbs held and pinned by his so that she must look like a starfish. She felt his breath in her hair and she struggled weakly with him. 'Let me go!' she implored. 'Please, Duane!'

'What is it?' he gibed. 'Are you afraid of my intentions? Was that why you ran away from me?'

'You frightened me – I ran without thinking.'

'Do I frighten you now?'

'You're hurting me,' she said. But it wasn't quite the truth. Though he had her pinned against the palm tree, her hands were within his and shielded from the scaly trunk. Though he was close enough for her to feel the lift and fall of his chest, the wool of his sweater was chunky and warm ... warm, drugging, so that quite irrationally she wanted to rest her churning head against him and be lost in the woolly blackness.

Their eyes clung and afraid he would guess how weak she was in that moment, she looked quickly away from him towards the lake, glinting darkly through the trees.

'What are you doing down here?' he demanded. 'Moon walking?'

'I – came to be alone. To think, and to try and find myself,' she said huskily, 'and here by this lake I remembered a lake in England – where I used to go swimming with someone—' Suddenly she was trembling, and on the point of tears. 'It was a girl! Not Armand at all, but a girl I used to know—'

She felt the hot welling of her tears and no longer cared that Duane should see them. The lake shimmered through her tears, and then his hand moved up her shoulder to her nape, enclosing its hollowed slenderness as he made her look at him. His lean face was moon-touched, his eyes intent upon her face. 'Who was the girl?' he asked. 'Do you remember her name?'

Roslyn shook her head and a tear spilled down her cheek. 'I – I wish I could remember.'

'Could the girl have been – Juliet Grey?'

'Juliet?' She shied from the question as lightning flickered along the shore. No! It seemed too terrible to think of that fair, laughing girl as dead ... killed in the plane crash. And yet it was obvious from what she remembered of those midnight dips in that English lake that she and the silvery-haired girl had been good friends.

It was at that point that the sky above was riven by lightning. It stabbed down towards the palm trees, and Duane wrenched her from the trunk and, her hand locked in his, ran her out into the open, away from the trees. The rain came down in a sheet and within seconds they were soaked.

'We must find somewhere to shelter while this lasts.' He glanced about him. 'Look, there's a shed of some sort – come on!'

Their feet sank in the wet sand as they ran, pursued by flashes of lightning and thunder that sounded as though Zeus was rolling his wine-casks for a long, stormy 'party'. They reached the door of what turned out to be a boat-shed; the lightning followed them in, revealing a couple of punts on their sides, coils of rope, a pile of canvas sails, some oars, and shelves of paint and tackle.

Duane pushed a hand into the hip pocket of his trousers and produced a lighter. He flicked it on and played the small light round the crowded shed, which smelled strongly of paint and tar. The small flame flickered, as though about to go out, and something made a whirring sound overhead.

'It's only a bat,' he said crisply. 'Ah, we're in luck for some illumination! A lamp!'

It was a small kerosene lamp and when he shook it, oil swished in the bottom of it. He took off the glass chimney and lit the wick. He was looking over at Roslyn as he replaced the chimney.

The rain had plastered her shirt to her like Regency muslin, and her hair lay on her forehead in wet spikes. She was shivering a little, wet, cold, and nervous under Duane's scrutiny.

He stepped across one of the punts and came to her. 'You seem to have got wetter than I did,' he said, feeling her shirt, either not noticing, or caring very much, that she shrank from his touch.

'You can't shiver in that wet shirt for the next hour – or two.' With a quick, lithe movement he peeled off the black sweater that had replaced his dinner jacket and felt it between his hands. 'You can wear this, the rain hasn't penetrated the wool – heavens, child, your teeth are chattering like castanets! Get that shirt off, pronto, or you'll take a chill.'

She stood by the boat-shed door, the rain pounding on the roof overhead, and though she recognized the sense in what he said, she couldn't do as he asked. She could only shake and feel wretched.

'There are two things in a female that really get my goat, mock-modesty and stubbornness. Here – catch!' He threw her the sweater, which she caught automatically. 'I'll turn my back while you take off that shirt – and you'd better take it off, Miss Prim, unless you want me to whip it off for you.'

She shivered, and saw his eyes narrow to jade slits as he swung away from her and stood lighting himself a cheroot. Her fingers shook on the buttons of her shirt; she dragged it off, pushed her arms into the sleeves of the sweater and dropped the garment down over her head. It was still warm from his body, smoky, with a faint male tang clinging to the black wool. It fell loosely to her hips, concealing her girl's body and giving her the look of an urchin in grown-up clothing.

She was laying her shirt out to dry on the hull of one of the boats when Duane turned to take stock of her. 'Great Scott!' Grin lines slashed his cheeks. 'You were kidding yourself, thinking I'd lose my control over a scrap like you. I have my standards, Miss Brant, for all my jungle upbringing.'

Yes, she thought, a picture of Isabela springing into her mind, a long curving leg revealed under her robe as she strolled out of *his* bedroom.

'Surely this storm will let up soon,' she said.

'It hardly seems likely.' Lightning flared outside the boat-shed window as he spoke, and thunder seemed to rock the foundations of the nearby cliffs. 'Surely you've realized by now that our desert climate, like our emotions, is never moderate?'

'I'm beginning to realize it.' She perched on the hull of the boat where her shirt was spread, her fingers ruffling the damp hair at her temples, feeling the warmth of his chunky sweater seeping into her bones. 'I hope you aren't missing your sweater,' she added.

He leaned against one of the stripped palm-pillars that supported the roof of the boat-shed, his cheroot smoke wafting up about his green eyes. He had a sleek, dangerous sort of strength, bristling in the copper hair, controlled but apparent in every hard line of him. A disturbing man!

'I'm used to climatic extremes,' he replied. 'You'd be amazed how cold it can become in the desert at certain times of year, mainly at night and towards dawn. Our sun is a hot one, but the actual climate is surprisingly cool. You could say,' he glanced lazily at the burning tip of his cheroot, 'that in many respects the desert is like a woman.'

'What, not easy to know, or temperate, with sometimes an inclination to be cool?' Her flippancy was a defence mechanism, switched on because they were alone in a storm and she could feel his sweater against her skin like a warm, rough touch.

'Those reasons, among others,' he agreed. 'Anything might crop up in the desert, as in a relationship with a woman.'

'And you, Mr. Hunter, prefer to deal with the moods of the desert rather than those of a woman?'

'Yes,' his mouth pulled to one side in a sardonic smile, 'as a matter of fact I do. A man can enjoy the desert without getting involved – emotionally.'

'Does Isabela share your sentiments?'

It wasn't until the words were out that Roslyn fully realized their import. Duane didn't move, and yet his white shirt seemed to tighten against the muscles that strapped his chest and shoulders. Then dropping his cheroot butt to the floor he ground it out beneath his heel.

'Why,' he drawled, 'should Isabela share my sentiments?'

Roslyn found it difficult to meet his eyes; unwavering jade eyes agleam with mockery. 'I'm not a schoolgirl,' she said defiantly. 'I know that a man and a beautiful woman don't discuss the weather – or the desert – when they're alone together in his – bedroom.'

'What do they do?' he asked deliberately.

Colour rushed up her neck into her face. His affair with Isabela was none of her business and it was a wonder he was looking – well, almost amused instead of angry. 'I'm sorry,' she said. 'You must think me very impertinent.'

She looked away from him, the bones of her neck showing fragile against the black wool of his sweater.

'Yes, you're impertinent,' he agreed. 'It's a fault of the young to rush in where angels fear to tread, and one that should be corrected.'

She gazed back at him, struck by a note in his voice that made her go tense. He had moved and was coming towards her, his shadow towering up the wall in the lamplight. A draught blew like cobwebs against her cheek, thunder cracked overhead, and then she felt the grip of his hands and was being swung bodily off the hull of the boat.

'No – you mustn't!' she gasped.

'Mustn't what?' As she dangled in his arms like a doll, he looked down into her eyes, enormous with her alarm. 'Spank you, or kiss you?'

'Oh – I hate you! Put me down!'

'Not until you take your choice,' he taunted. 'Shall I spank that pert little behind of yours, or shall I kiss those indiscreet pink lips?'

'You – you wouldn't dare—'

'I'd dare both, and you know it.' He laughed unkindly, gave her backside a light clip and set her down near the door. 'Now stay there a moment, you hasty female. As it happens I didn't grab hold of you in order to slake a sudden passion – my intentions were never more honourable, as you will soon see.'

Still laughing, he took a stride back to the boat on which she had been sitting and peered hard at something embedded in a web that had been empty when she had first sat down. It was a large black spider with crooked legs – a repulsive hairy thing that sent a thrill of horror through Roslyn.

'I don't think it's venomous,' Duane said quietly. 'I thought it was when I first caught sight of the beauty. Do they scare you?'

'It's beastly,' she whispered. 'I'd have died if – if I'd known it was that close to me.'

'Do you want me to despatch it?' he asked.

'C-couldn't you put it in a tin and throw it out of the window?'

'Soft-hearted about a spider?' he jeered, but for a brief moment he turned to look at her and those mocking eyes of his were more tawny than green. 'Have a look on that shelf for an empty paint tin, and a dry brush. Hurry, child. Our hairy friend is beginning to stir and I don't want to lose him.'

She didn't want that either, and she quickly stepped over the boat tackle lying about on the floor, climbed on to the pile of canvas sails and searched along the shelf of paint tins for one that would serve their purpose. To her relief she found one with about an inch of dried paint in it, and also a piece of stick that had probably been used for stirring turpentine. She jumped down off the sails and approached Duane with caution. 'Here you are,' she said, keeping her eyes averted from the spider.

'Thanks. Now go and stand by the door while I pop our friend in the can.'

Roslyn didn't need to be told twice, her nails digging into her palms as with a deft flick of the stick Duane ejected the tenant of the web and clapped a hand over the top of the tin. He then suggested that Roslyn open the door for him because it might take longer to open the window and he could feel the spider tickling his fingers.

She knew at once that he still wasn't certain whether the thing had a venomous bite or not – instantly she threw open the door and stood back so that he could hurl the tin and its occupant far into the rainswept night.

'And you call me reckless!' she exclaimed.

He grinned down at her, rain in the grooves of his face and one large drop running down a lance of his copper hair. It plopped on to Roslyn's face and she drew back a little from him.

'I was giving Beelzebub the benefit of the doubt,' he said.

'Well, that's more than you ever gave me, Mr. Hunter.' She was retreating so he could close the door, when there was a sudden loud rumbling noise. It wasn't thunder. It was as though a ton of coal was being shot down the face of the cliffs!

The rumbling went on for more than a minute, then it slithered into silence ... a silence broken by one or two muddy thumps.

'Whatever was that?' Roslyn whispered.

'A landslide.' He spoke curtly. 'Unless I'm very much mistaken, half the cliffs have slid down on to the shore.'

He brushed past her into the boat-shed, grabbed the hurricane lamp and hastened out into the rain. Roslyn followed without thinking of the storm, as anxious as Duane to find out how bad the landslide was.

Wires of unease were knotting inside her as she ran along beside him. Lances of lightning and shadow crossed their path like foils, and soon they were squelching through mud and Duane was warning her to watch out for large pieces of rock that could twist her ankle in an instant.

She knew without being told that he was making for the path that led down from the cliffs, and she prayed they would find it intact and that they would be able to get back to the shelter and safety of the hotel. It had been crazy, venturing down here in the first place. The things she remembered made her feel more mixed up in her mind than ever.

'Duane, what were you doing down here?' The question had been in her mind for the past half hour, and she didn't know why she asked him now, as they ploughed along in the mud and rain.

'I was taking a stroll,' he yelled above the rumble of thunder. 'Did you think I followed you?'

She cast an indignant sideglance at him just as the lake seemed to ripple with white fire. It threw Duane's tall figure into relief, magnifying in its glare his wide, aggressive shoulders and pagan head.

'Of course not,' she yelled back, knowing full well that while she had been on her way down here, he had been with Isabela ... discussing deception and how much he disliked people who played such a game.

She was getting out of breath, falling behind Duane and stumbling over lumps of rock that had fallen from the cliffs, a warning that they were close to where the landslide had occurred.

Duane was several yards ahead of her by now, playing the light of the lamp up the cliffside. 'Angels weep!' she heard him exclaim. 'The whole path is a chute of mud and rock. Come and take a look!'

In her anxiety to take a look she hastened her pace without taking due care. Here the ground was not only littered with boulders, but the rain had turned the piles of fallen soil into puddles of slippery mud. Roslyn ran right into one of these and was thrown off her feet in an instant, landing painfully and awkwardly on her right shoulder. She lay stunned, the rain splashing down on her, and the pain of her shoulder making it impossible for her to rise from the ground for a moment or two. She was making the effort when Duane reached her side. He caught hold of her with his free hand. 'What have you gone and done?' he demanded, for she was unable to suppress a small groan.

'I – fell over in the mud. M-my shoulder hurts.'

He played the lamp over her pale face and muddy figure, then he set it down on the ground and explored her shoulder with a careful hand.

'Ouch!' she said.

'I know it's painful,' he growled, 'but you haven't broken anything. Why the devil didn't you take more care?'

'I – I wanted to see how bad a state the path is in. Is it *very* bad?'

'I'm afraid so. The mud that just tumbled you is some indication of the state that path is in. Trying to climb it would be madness. It's like a chute of wet black ice, peppered with rocks. Using the rocks for handholds wouldn't work. The mud has probably loosened them and we'd only pull them right out.'

'But—' the breath was shocked out of her. 'But we can't stay down here *all night*.'

'We'll spend the night in the boat-shed,' he said firmly. 'It would be lunacy to attempt that climb. There might be another fall and we'd be buried under a cascade of mud and rocks.'

'You'd risk it if you were alone,' she flared, trembling from the pain of her wrenched shoulder, almost weeping with her need to wash off all this mud and climb into a clean, warm bed.

'I might,' he agreed. 'But at the moment I am not alone. I'm stuck with you, you little hellion, and we're both going to have to make the best of it until morning. The mud will dry as soon as the sun gets up. Now back to the boat-shed, young lady.'

'I'm not going back.'

'You are, my girl.' He picked up the lamp and caught

124

at her left arm. She struggled to get away from his grip, tears starting to her eyes at the pain she caused herself.

'Now don't make things worse than they are already,' he chided her. 'The boat-shed is dry and we're both getting soaked to the skin out here in the open. If you want a cold or a fever, I don't! Now be a sensible girl, before I lose my temper.'

'Lose it!' she blazed. 'I shall feel more at home with you if you're cutting and sarcastic. I'm more used to that than the "good scout" treatment. I prefer it.'

'You little fool—' then even as his hand tightened on her arm, lightning zigzagged across the lake, lighting up the mess that lay at the foot of the cliffs, and forking into the heart of a nearby palm tree. There was a fearful rending noise, then before the appalled eyes of Roslyn the tree exploded into flame from top to bottom.

'Come on, let's get out of this!' And not waiting for further argument, he hooked a sinewy arm around her waist and hoisted her right off the ground. The mud squelched under his long strides and he made it to the gaping door of the boat-shed in about four minutes. He marched in, still carrying Roslyn like a rag doll, and kicked the door shut behind them. The door rattled on its hinges as he released her and they stood looking at one another in the flickering lamplight.

'You poor scrap, if you could see yourself!' He put back his head, dark and rough with rain, and his laughter filled the room.

'You look like one of hell's angels yourself,' she snapped back. Then wincing with the pain of her shoulder she sagged against one of the palm supports and wiped the rain from her face with her hand. 'The way that tree burst into flame,' she said, shuddering. 'It reminded me of the plane when it crashed – the way it lit up from end to end, a-and then seemed to buckle with its own pain. I saw that – just before I passed out—'

'How's your shoulder?' he turned from putting the lamp on a shelf. His eyes flicked her face, peaky under the streaks of mud. 'Carrying you like a sack of oats couldn't have helped, but you were acting like a stubborn little jackass.'

'Thanks,' she retorted. 'You certainly have a delightful way of speaking to a girl.'

'Don't you like it?' He arched a mocking eyebrow. 'I've met females who really go for that line. They consider the insult a prelude to seduction.'

'No wonder you're cynical about women, if that's the type you're used to mixing with.' She tilted her chin scornfully, though she felt a spasm of nervousness as she took in his rain-ruffled hair above the captive devils in his eyes; his wet shirt moulded to the hard bone and sinew of him.

Outside the rain hammered cold steel bars around this shelter on the shore ... she was intolerably alone with Duane Hunter, a savage, unpredictable man.

'Why,' he drawled, 'do women always assume there is a hidden meaning in all male remarks?'

'*All* women don't assume any such thing. Ugh!' She pulled the wet wool of his sweater away from her neck. 'How I'd love a hot shower right now, and a huge warm towel to dry myself on.'

'Me, too,' he growled, grimacing down at the mud caking his shoes and the legs of his trousers. 'With a mulled rum-punch to follow.'

'I wouldn't say no to a big cup of coffee, all steamy and sweet.'

'Instead, child, we are going to have to make the most of what we've got.' He frowned and studied the pile of canvas sails, then he looked at Roslyn, slumped slim and tousled against the palm support, her teeth clenching her bottom lip.

'Is the shoulder paining you?' he asked.

'It is a bit sickening,' she admitted. 'I think I must have wrenched it.'

'Here, let me see what I can do to ease it – now don't jib away from me like a nervous filly!'

'Well, you're always so rough—'

'You think me a pretty unfeeling sort, eh?'

'Yes, unfeeling – not exactly pretty.' She met his eyes, green shot with devil's gold. She felt him peel the soggy sweater up over her shoulders and he began to massage her neck where it joined her shoulder, gently but deeply. His hands were warm, the skin calloused from years of working among trees ... all sorts of trees and soils and their fruits.

'The Indians might be primitive,' he said, 'but they know a whole lot about the human body. Indian women do this for their children when they tumble out of trees – there, that's the spot, isn't it?'

'Mmmm,' he was making her sleepy, that large, warm, calloused hand on her neck, her shoulder, her spinal column. The ache was receding ... and there was an uncanny silence all round that mystified her. Then she realized that the rain had died away. The storm was over, but she and Duane would have to stay here in the boatshed until morning.

'There,' his breath ruffled the hair at her temples, 'how does that feel? Easier?'

'Heaps better. Thank you for the osteopathy.' Now he wasn't touching her she felt suddenly conscious of the updrawn sweater and drew it down quickly.

'You'd better not keep that on all night,' he said, frowning. 'Maybe I can cut you a piece of that canvas to wrap round yourself, like a sarong. It is dry – h'm, let's see if there's a knife handy, or a pair of scissors.'

He stepped across the punts and boat tackle and began to search the cluttered shelves. The flame of the lamp was smoking, as though the oil was running low, and Roslyn thought tiredly that she had been wrong about his lack of feeling. He could feel for others and be kind in his own brusque fashion.

His wet shirt, she noticed, was drying on him. Though he was tough as his own trees, it couldn't feel very comfortable. She shifted a sandalled foot forward, then back. She wanted to suggest that he remove the shirt, but she didn't know how to say it without sounding . . . provocative.

A bubble of laughter rose in her throat and escaped.

'What's funny?' He glanced round inquiringly.

'Nothing – well, as a matter of fact I was wondering how to suggest you take off your wet shirt without sounding as though I'd like to see your muscles. Please take it off. You did mention something about fever—'

'Fever? Oh, sure, that's a legacy most jungle planters collect.' He tugged the shirt out of the band of his trousers and whipped it off. When he turned again to the shelves, the smoky lamplight played over his upper body, revealing the pale outline of a scar that jagged across his right shoulder, deep in the brown muscles. An animal must have caused it, she thought. A jaguar hiding in a tree, leaping down when his back was turned and rending his body . . . as that woman he had known had rended him on the inside. Turning him into the type of man whose kindness had to be counter-balanced by hardness. . . .

She had seen the muscles ridging his jaw when he had briefly turned to look at her. He had flung down his shirt as though, all at once, this whole situation irritated him.

CHAPTER TEN

HE had found something sharp and was ripping at the canvas . . . rip, rip, cutting the silence like a lash.

'I'm sorry to have put you to all this trouble,' Roslyn said, wincing.

'Being sorry after the deed isn't much good! This canvas will feel a bit coarse, but it will keep you warm, and preserve your modesty. Do you know how to wrap yourself in a sarong?'

'No.' His tone of voice had stung. 'But I am sure you do, Mr. Hunter, being such a ladies' man.'

He slewed round to look at her, copper-hard as an Indian in the lamplight, his brows meeting in a dark ridge above his green-gold eyes. 'Worried that I won't behave like a gentleman?' He gave an unkind laugh as his eyes took her in from head to foot. 'I only wish there was a mirror in this place so you could see what you look like. A half-drowned young cat comes nearest to it. Here you are, pussy, do you want me to show you how to wrap a sarong?'

'I'll manage,' she said, snatching the length of sailcloth from him and giving him her most withering look. He returned it, with interest, then presented his back to her and proceeded to unroll more of the canvas.

'We'll bed down on this,' he said without looking round. 'We might as well make further use of it. How are you managing?'

By now she had his damp sweater off and was wrapping the canvas around her . . . more like a toga, she knew, than a glamorous sarong. 'All right,' she said, stepping out of her trews.

'May I turn round and receive the full benefit of the

seductive picture you must make?' he asked sardonically.

'Is there any need for you to be so – so nasty?' she inquired. 'I didn't ask to be stranded in a boat-shed with you. I'd sooner risk that climb to the headland than stay here.'

'I'm sure of it.' He turned round lazily, flicking his eyes over her, a corner of his mouth quirking with amusement. 'Pussy, you wouldn't exactly qualify as a South Seas model for Gauguin – look, tuck that free end in just above your bosom. That's the ticket! Now you don't have to hang on to the garment for dear life. D'you feel comfortable?'

'About as comfortable as a flea in the fire,' she said witheringly. 'It may not worry you, being stranded down here like this, but I – I don't like it. People are going to think it – odd.'

'By people, I take it you mean Tristan?' An eyebrow followed the quirk of his mouth. 'My dear child, he knows me well enough to be certain I wouldn't touch a hair of your head.'

'I'm sure Tristan knows your tastes,' she retorted. 'But women aren't quite so tolerant as men.'

'By women, I presume you mean Isabela?'

She nodded, holding the front of the canvas toga, though it was now secured, and feeling as gauche as she was certain she looked.

He studied her, his eyes narrowed, then he resumed his task of fixing them a couch for the night. His back muscles rippled as he shifted boat tackle to one side, making room for one of the punts to be hoisted and righted. He then took hold of the lamp, spluttering and darkening by the minute, and played its smoky light from stem to stern of the punt. It wasn't harbouring any spiders and, with his profile looking haughty in the lamplight, he lined the punt with canvas sails.

'We should rest in this quite comfortably,' he said to

Roslyn. 'You can take one end, I'll take the other. Okay?'

'Yes, Mr. Hunter.' She spoke in a more subdued voice, for it had to be admitted that he was a resourceful man. The canvas-lined punt did look more inviting than the floor.

'We'd better get into our gondola before the lamp goes out. Upsadaisy!' He lifted her over the side. 'When I get in at the other end, I'll pull more of the canvas over us. Settle down, I'm just going to spread out my shirt and sweater. They should be dry by the morning.'

She curled down in the bottom of the punt and watched him lay his two garments alongside her shirt, trews, and muddy sandals. The lamp was spluttering out as he stepped over the side of the punt, which rocked as it took his weight. Roslyn was relieved when she heard him toss his shoes to the floor; being so tall his feet would rest alongside her face when he stretched out to sleep.

She heard him yanking more of the canvas over the side. 'Don't be nervous about tucking it around you,' he said. 'I had a good look in case anything was lurking in the folds. Wow, it doesn't feel exactly like the best linen, does it? Never mind, it will keep us warm.' His long legs came slithering down beside her. 'Are my feet anywhere near your face?' he wanted to know.

She felt them with her hand. 'I hope you don't kick,' she said.

'Lord knows. It would be better if we were both – look, I'll try and move up under the stern seat – *ouch*!'

'What have you done?' she called out.

'Given myself a black eye, I think.' Then she heard him chuckle and guessed the bump wasn't *that* serious. 'A shiner would cause comment up at the hotel in the morning, eh?'

Isabela would probably match it with another, she thought tartly.

She listened while he settled down, and though they

weren't touching she could feel him with her nerves. Outside in the damp darkness tree frogs seemed to croak a question; the lake water whispered and the palm leaves joined in sibilantly.

'Asleep yet?' His voice made a low thunder in the dusk.

'No.' She nestled her cheek on her hand. 'I'm wooing it.'

'Sorry I don't know any lullabies. There was one my Indian nanny used to croon to me when I was a nipper, but it would probably sound rather odd to you.'

'I bet you were as wild as an Indian when you were a boy,' she said drowsily.

'That was inevitable, especially when—' there he broke off and Roslyn felt him shift restlessly. 'It's funny . . . love, I mean. Love of a place as much as for a person. It gets into your bones.'

'Do you wish you had never left the jungle?' she asked.

'I'm not talking about myself,' he said after a moment.

'I thought—'

'No. Jungle life was an experience I wouldn't have missed for the world, but I never felt as deeply about it all as my father did. For him it was home, purpose and playground. It was his life.'

Roslyn knew from conversations with Nanette that Duane was a reticent man when it came to his personal affairs, and she was duly surprised that he should talk to her about his father. Was it their strange surroundings which induced this mood of amity? The darkness masked them from each other, and perhaps he also felt that if he talked about his father she would feel less nervous of being so intimately alone with him.

'It must have been hard for him to leave,' she said. 'Nanette told me that he returned to England and that was why you agreed to take charge of the plantation at Dar al Amra.'

'He was sick, tired. Much as he loved the jungle, many

more months of it would have killed him and in the end he agreed to retire to Loughboys, a small riverside house left to him in Kent by his brother.'

Duane fell silent, and the frogs in the trees went on croaking their question.

'You're tired,' he said in a moment. 'You must want to sleep.'

'It's the kind of tiredness that won't let me sleep, just yet,' she replied. 'If you want to talk, I'd like to listen.'

'Like kids in a dormitory, eh?'

'Yes,' she said. Kids in the dormitory of an orphanage. She couldn't yet remember the orphanage, the place where she and Juliet Grey had grown up. But orphanages were cold places. She had never known the warmth of a close relationship with a parent, and she wanted Duane to talk to her about his father.

'How is your father settling down in England?' she asked.

'Better than I'd hoped. His letters are far more cheerful than they used to be – I wanted him to join me at Dar al Amra a couple of years back, but he wouldn't come out. He said the place held memories for him that he just couldn't face. He stuck it out at Loughboys, and now he seems to have found compensations there. It is a place you could grow fond of.'

'You've been there?' Somehow she couldn't imagine him in a quiet country setting.

'I took leave and went home with my father when he retired. Loughboys hadn't been lived in for some time and it needed painting and redecorating. We did all that ourselves, then pruned out the orchard at the back of the house, and built a large hen-coop for the pullets and cockerels he wanted to breed. It was all very different from what he'd always cared for. Different for me, too. A Tudor house with a timber porch and honeysuckle climbers arching over it. The smell of gorse, and hops drying in the oast-kilns. Church bells across fields, where barley-beards shook in the wind.

'I knew it would take him a devil of a time to settle down, and I offered to stay on in England, to get a job there. But he wouldn't hear of it. If a man sacrificed the work he loved, he said, in the end he shrivelled as a man and became no use to anyone. But the jungle wasn't the same without him, and I jumped at the chance Nanette offered me. Fresh surroundings, doing the work I was trained to do, and wanted to do.'

Duane was silent a moment, then he added: 'The jungle held memories for me, the sort I could no longer face. I – don't suppose I shall ever go back there.'

He didn't say any more, and Roslyn assumed that he had fallen off to sleep. Snug under the warm canvas, she thought about the last few hours and all that had happened since Duane had forced her to stumble round that dance floor. How she had hated him. Now ... now she didn't know what to make of him.

Perplexed, her eyelids weighted, she drifted off to sleep and everything fell quiet.

The morning sun struck through the boat-shed window. It moved gradually across the shed until it dwelt, like a startled eye, upon the girl and the man at either end of one of the punts. The man slept with his face buried on a bare brown arm. The girl was beginning to stir. A minute or so later her eyes opened and she was blinking at the sun.

Where on earth ...?

She struggled into a sitting position and took in her surroundings ... her sleeping companion.

It was the stiffness of her shoulder that brought back last night's adventure with a rush. There had been a violent storm, with torrential rain, and lightning so bad it had blasted a palm tree. The cliff-path to the hotel had been all but swept away, and Duane had said they must stay down here until morning.

Now it was morning, and it was so good to see the sun and hear birds whistling outside. She flexed her shoulder-blades, then slipped out of the punt, careful not to disturb Duane before she had put on her trews and her shirt. The shirt was the drip-dry sort, but her trews still felt a bit tacky. She zipped the waist of them, and studied Duane before she had put on her trews and her shirt. He would awake any second now, but despite this she took a step closer to the punt and saw with wonderment how sleep robbed him of his aggressiveness, tamed him ... made a boy of him, almost.

His profile seemed less fierce, but that was because his eyes were closed and his lips a little open as he breathed in sleep. Then, as the sunlight shafted across his eyes and he began to stir, she turned and made for the door. She unlatched it and went outside.

A morning mist hung over the lake, but already the sun was warm and drying out the puddles left by the rain. She went to the edge of the lake, knelt down and scooped water into her palms. She washed her face as best she could and after dabbing it dry with her handkerchief, dipped a corner of the cambric in the water and gave her teeth a makeshift scrub. She had no comb with her and used her fingers to get the tangles out of her hair.

She must still look bedraggled, but it couldn't be helped.

A smell of mud and wrack hung on the morning air, and she guessed from the noise the birds were making that it was still very early. They winged from the shore to that green island in the centre of the lake, large birds and smaller ones that sped through the air like coloured arrows.

She watched them for a few minutes, then made her way back to the boat-shed, where she found Duane fold-ing and re-stacking the canvas they had made use of. 'G-good morning,' she said a trifle nervously. 'Can I do anything to help?'

'No, I'm almost through.' And as she watched, he heaved the punt back into position for repairs to its planking, dusted off his hands on the sides of his trousers and pulled on his sweater. Gone was that air of boyishness while he slept. With his unshaven chin and untidy copper hair he looked like a desperado, and she found herself backing out of the shed as he came towards her, his shirt in his hand.

'The ends of your hair are wet,' he said. 'Had a cat's lick and a promise in the lake?'

She nodded, thrust her hands into the pockets of her trews and put on a nonchalant air. His voice had struck her as curt, his eyes as she met them were a cool green. He was armoured again, and the naturalness and ease between them was gone with the storm, the night, the putting in order of the strange sleeping quarters they had shared.

He took a look along the shore, littered forlornly with broken branches, palm fronds and bird nests. The sun was spreading, dispelling the mist over the lake, and crusting the mud pools. 'I'll just splash my face, then we'll take a look at the cliff-path and see about getting back to the hotel.'

'Yes,' she said. 'What is the time?'

He glanced at his wristwatch, the leather strap only a shade darker than his sun-tanned skin. 'Five-forty,' he said, and she saw his lip quirk with that smile that wasn't kind. 'We might manage to get back before we're missed. You're anxious for that, eh?'

'What's the odds?' She tilted her chin and hoped she looked braver than she felt. 'Some of the hotel staff are bound to see us.'

'They might think we were on our way back to the hotel

after taking a look at the landslide,' he pointed out.

'Of course,' she said doubtfully. 'I didn't think of that.'

'Then again,' his laugh was sardonic, 'neither of us look as though we've slept anything but rough. You look as though you fell in a pond and had to be fished out and dried off in the sun. What I look like probably doesn't dare description.'

She swept her eyes over him, nettled. 'You look as though you pushed me in the pond in the first place,' she flashed.

'Temper, temper,' he chided her, then he swung about and crunched storm-wrack and drying sand under his shoes as he strode to the lake-edge. There he flung handfuls of water over his hair and his face, and dried off on the shirt that had once looked so crisp and white under his dinner-jacket. He threw it carelessly to one side, and as he rejoined Roslyn he flattened his hair with his palms. Hair as truculent and unmanageable as he was, the colour of brush-fire as the sun touched it.

'That feels better, but I could go something to eat.' He narrowed his eyes in self-torturing speculation. 'A large plate of crisp-fried whitebait, with a stack of brown bread and butter, and a pot of coffee on the side. How does that sound?'

'Sadistic,' she rejoined. 'Mr. Hunter, let me point out that the sooner we climb that cliffside, the sooner we will both get our breakfast.'

'That path was in a pretty awful mess last night, and climbing it this morning isn't going to be a picnic. I may decide to climb it alone – now don't flash those grey eyes at me! If I say you stay down here a while longer, then you stay. I'll get some help, and ropes to haul you up.'

'I'm not helpless,' she stormed. 'I'll climb that cliffside if it's safe enough for you, and you won't stop me.'

'You think not?' He thrust his hands into his trouser pockets and stood looking down at her. 'Obstinacy I can

137

take because I happen to be that way myself, but you have another reason for wanting to get back into that hotel without anyone knowing about our little adventure. You're afraid of what Tristan will think. To him you're the little girl who hasn't long trumbled out of the peach tree, and you don't want to spoil his charming picture.'

'You – you cruel devil!' She swung her hand at his jaw, but swiftly he caught and gripped it.

'It wouldn't occur to you, puss, that you're being unkind yourself, not to say a little cruel.' Now he held both her hands, and his teeth showed in a faint, thin smile as he gazed down at her, taking in the flushes high on her cheekbones, and the furious blaze in her eyes.

'You and Tristan saw Isabela leaving my bedroom yesterday afternoon,' he went on. 'You both assumed I had been making love to her, and you've got it into your head that Tristan will think there was a repeat performance last night, with you as the leading lady. Am I right?'

The flushes deepened in her cheeks. 'Why do you say I – I'm being cruel?'

'You women don't like to be told that, do you?' His smile was grimly amused. 'It upsets even the most hardened, I've noticed. Well, if it will set your mind at rest with regard to what Tristan may think of our night alone in the boat-shed, I'll tell you what Isabela was really doing in my room. We weren't long back from lunch, which she insisted on having at a rooftop café, and I was about to take a snooze when she knocked on my door. The sunshine had given her a headache and she had nothing to take for it – could I provide? When you've lived under the sun as long as I have you learn to be wary of the orb and – like some Aunt Polly – I always carry remedies for headaches, the collywobbles, and attacks of fever.

'I mixed a headache dose for Isabela and she drank it in my room. She was on her way to her own room to sleep it off when you and Tristan appeared on the scene and saw her, seductively clad in a *peignoir*, leaving me with her hair down her back. It was plain what you were thinking, Miss Puss.'

He took Roslyn by the chin and tilted her face. 'I didn't set you right last night because I wanted you to think my type of girl strictly Latin. It was something new for me, the care and protection of a kid for the night, and I didn't want you to get the idea that I found you – appealing.'

'I – I've never made *that* mistake,' she protested.

'No, but you were quick to think my cousin would assume that I found you irresistible.'

'Well, unlike you,' Roslyn blushed, 'he – likes me.'

'And liking someone goes hand in hand with jealousy, eh?'

She nodded. 'Human nature being what it is.'

'Our human natures are a problem, aren't they?' he said dryly. 'We're all mysteries, to ourselves and each other. If we weren't, you would have accepted me as a sort of big brother last night and not given the matter a second thought.'

'The trouble is,' she gave a rueful laugh, 'you don't look like anyone's big brother.'

'How do I look, in your opinion?'

Like thunder and lightning, she thought swiftly. Like all the things that belong in jungles and deserts.

'You're rather formidable, and you know it,' she rejoined. 'You haven't Tristan's gift, or your grandmother's, for putting people at their ease.'

'I'm sorry about that,' his smile was wry. 'But you've got to remember that I'm a mongrel. Crossing a French bitch with a British bulldog was bound to produce someone like me. But my bark, you know, is apt to be worse than my bite, at times.'

She smiled, but deep inside she was shocked by something in his remark that wasn't funny. Her eyes dwelt on him, wide and curious, and abruptly he let go of her and said it was time they were taking a look at the cliff-path.

He strode on ahead of her, and when she caught up with him he was scanning the wrecked path, the exposed roots of bushes and loose rocks. The sun had climbed higher and behind them the lake had a metallic sheen. There was a buzz of tiny insects, drawn in swarms to the mud and vegetation drying out on the shore, and Roslyn aimed self-defensive slaps at herself as she watched Duane knocking the looser rocks free of the caked mud.

She didn't care what decision he arrived at with regard to the safety of the climb. She wasn't staying down here to be eaten alive by sand-flies!

'Let's take a chance,' she said. 'I shall be covered in bites before very long.'

He cast her a look over his shoulder. 'All right,' he said. 'But I shall go ahead and I expect you to take every step I take. Understand?'

'I'm not a child.' She beat off a persistent fly from the side of her neck. 'Please, let's get going! These flies are a pest, and I'm dying for a cup of coffee and a wash.'

'It's a good job we aren't starting a trek through the jungle.' He smiled derisively. 'These flies are ladybirds in comparison to the sort you have to contend with there.'

'I'm sure they are,' she said tartly. 'But I imagine I'd be wearing protective clothing of some sort.'

'Do you want to wear my sweater?' he asked.

'It's miles too big for me – *ouch*!' she slapped hard at her leg. 'It might hamper my movements.'

'It probably would,' he agreed. 'Now look, I want you to hold on to my belt as we climb,' he showed her the belt under his sweater. 'Hold on hard, and don't try anything that I don't.'

'Aye, aye, skipper.' She grinned jauntily enough, but the rough-stepped path she had descended last night was gone and in its place was a steep, hazardous climb up the

140

cliffside. Here and there large boulders jutted out. If one of them tore loose and crashed down on Duane and herself, they would be badly hurt ... even killed.

'You know,' he said, 'you could go back to the boatshed for an hour or so. You would be free of sand-flies.'

'I'm not afraid to make the climb. You wouldn't be making it, Duane, if you thought it dangerous enough to cause you an injury. You like being strong and independent, and people who get hurt lose their strength and have to surrender themselves to the care of others.' She smiled knowingly. 'You wouldn't risk that.'

'Come on then, clever puss.' He swung to face the climb and reached up to test a claw of exposed roots. They held, and when Roslyn had slid a hand under and over his leather belt, he began to pick his way up the cliff-face.

They strained and braced and forced themselves upwards. One by one the fingernails of Roslyn's hands broke as she clung to Duane, and used the other hand to clutch at anything that offered. The sweat ran down her back, her feet felt bruised and her calves were aching. Every now and again Duane paused to give her a rest. Birds flew about them, curious and squawking.

'Oh, for the wings of a dove,' Roslyn panted.

'An eagle's would be of more use,' Duane threw back. 'I'd be able to whisk you up over that summit in my beak.'

The summit, now, was only a few yards away from where they clung like a pair of limpets to the cliffside. The sun was full on them, and Roslyn could feel his warm perspiring skin under her hand. When he began to climb again, she felt the muscles of his back, and followed doggedly where he led.

They were almost home and dry – Roslyn could all but taste that cup of coffee – when suddenly a rock broke loose under her feet and she slipped and hung suspended in space from Duane's belt.

He staggered as he took her weight, then lunged upwards and caught swiftly at some overhanging shrub. 'Try and grab me around the legs with your other arm,' he threw over his shoulder. 'That's it ... don't let go. Use me to lever yourself up ... there, are you making it?'

Obeying blindly, she gripped his left thigh and pulled herself in against him, kicking at the cliff for a foothold. She found one, thank heaven, and rested for a moment with her head against Duane's hip, her heart thumping in her chest, a lurid picture of the pair of them plummeting through the air, crashing over and over down the cliffside.

It had almost happened! Her full and unexpected weight on Duane's belt had very nearly jerked him away from the cliff.

'S-sorry about that,' she panted. 'It's a – a good thing your reactions are quick ones.'

'Force of habit,' he rejoined. 'Are you okay?'

'Yes, thank you. What about you? Your belt – it must have cut into you.'

'You aren't that heavy,' he chided her. 'Come on, we haven't much farther to go. You said you were dying for a cup of coffee and a wash, remember?'

'Putting it like that *was* tempting Providence.' She strove to speak lightly. 'All I want now is to reach that headland and have my feet on solid ground.'

They began the final lap of the climb, and at last they lay regaining their breath on the coarse grass of the headland. 'Well, we made it,' Duane said at last.

'Thanks to you.' She sat up and inspected her person. Her shirt was torn, her trews blotched by soil and mud, and her hair clustered sweatily at her temples and nape. She must look a wreck. Duane, beside her, looked more of a desperado than ever.

He jumped to his feet and gave her a hand up. 'You're spunky yourself.' He grinned and patted her cheek, as though she were a child. 'Now let's go and get that coffee.'

She glanced back once, before she followed him. Lake Temcina glittered, reflecting the shadows of birds. A place she would not forget ... unless when she awoke from her amnesia her memories of El Kadia faded like a dream.

When she caught up with Duane, he was inspecting his watch. 'It's still early,' he said. 'We may manage to sneak in without being seen.'

'Do you mean,' Roslyn took a breath, 'are *you* suggesting we don't tell anyone where we've been – all night?'

'Well, it isn't any of their business, is it?'

'But down on the shore – you said—'

'Forget what I said, down there.' The entrance of the hotel hove in sight, no signs of activity to be seen. 'You see, I've just realized something, up here.'

His eyes met Roslyn's, a startling green in his brown, unshaven face. 'I don't want Isabela to know about our little adventure – not if it can be avoided.'

And by some miracle of chance they did manage to get back to their rooms without being seen. Roslyn at once set about having a proper wash, and ten minutes later an Arab appeared at her door with a pot of coffee on a tray, a large cup and a small jug of cream.

Had Mr. Hunter ordered it for her? she asked as she took the tray. The Arab nodded, then bowed, and was gone.

Duane Hunter was certainly a puzzle, Roslyn thought, as she sipped her second cup of delicious coffee and pondered the events of their strange night together.

It could almost have been a dream, except that she still remembered the girl with the silvery hair and the gay laughter ... and her own tears, springing from a subconscious knowledge that her friend *had* died in the plane crash.

Poor, pretty thing, she would never again dance round the willow trees, the ends of her shoulder-length hair wet from their dip in the lake that was supposed to be out of bounds.

Her coffee finished, Roslyn stretched out on her bed, relishing its comfort after a night spent cramped in a punt beside a long pair of legs. She was no longer sure that it was wise to keep the adventure a secret. She and Duane would look far more guilty in the eyes of everyone if the secret leaked out later on.

CHAPTER ELEVEN

IN the days that followed Roslyn was glad that Duane was kept busy about the plantation and she saw him so infrequently. They shared a secret. They were conspirators. But the feeling this gave her was an uneasy one.

Tristan was busy with his opera most of the daytime. In the cool of the evening he had a couple of horses saddled and he and Roslyn took rides together. She had needed lessons, but he was a good instructor and soon she was at home in the saddle and able to enjoy the dusky desert all around them as they rode; also their discussions about his musical ambitions and his travels.

They wore the Arab cloaks that were not only picturesque, but warm. For both of them these hours alone on horseback were happy, companionable ones. *J'aime être avec vous*, they could say to each other with truth. I like being with you.

Roslyn thrust to the back of her mind her adventure with Duane. It suited both of them to forget the episode, and she was determined not to feel guilty about it. And she didn't feel guilty with the exotic beauty of the North African night all about her, doubly cloaking her. Strange vibrations seemed to pulse in the air, and her laughter joined Tristan's as he recited an anecdote from his life among singers, musicians and all those who created the drama and fantasy of a stage production.

'We of that world are all inclined to over-dramatize,' Tristan told her. 'Sometimes I wonder if we grow away from reality and become the heroes and heroines of opera. There is, you see, no other art form that exaggerates to such an extent the emotion of love, and the lengths to which jealousy and hatred can lead a person.'

'I can't remember if I have ever seen an opera,' she mused. 'I like your music and the way Isabela sings it. She has a superb voice.'

'A voice for declaiming all the emotions,' he agreed dryly. 'Yes, she has a great deal of vocal talent, and she is also an excellent actress.'

'Have you known her long?'

'About three years. We met in Paris while she was performing in *Carmen*. I had just completed *Ar Mor* and thought her perfect for the leading role. Fortunately she agreed with me, and I consider that *Ar Mor* achieved its overnight success because of her performance.'

'Do you also admire her as a person, Tristan?'

He shook his head. 'Not nearly as much as I admire you as a person,' he said frankly.

She flushed in the darkness. 'But you know so little about me,' she argued. 'I might be capable of anything – of deception, for instance.'

'Most women are,' he laughed, with a hint of Gallic cynicism. 'So are most men. It is a human condition, and one we must accept or remain friendless.'

She liked his answer. It withdrew the hook from her heart and allowed her to breathe again. 'You're a very mature and understanding person,' she said.

'That is because I am French,' he replied.

She studied him in the star-glow, not in the least Arab-looking in his cloak, though Duane in the same sort of garment looked a hawk of the desert.

'Do you intend to live in France one day?' she asked. 'You must love all this, the desert, the sense of freedom, the big icy stars.'

'El Kadia is in my blood to a certain extent,' he lifted his dark eyes to the stars and then let his gaze roam the shadowed sands, 'but Brittany is where I should like to settle down. I should like to buy a house near the sea, one with gables, a grapevine that clambers everywhere like

Jack's beanstalk, and big oaken doors set in rough-cast walls. The evenings in Brittany are warm and wild with the sound of the sea, and one eats spitted woodcock, roasted over the fire and smoke of vine roots, washed down with a *vin sauvage*. Or rock lobster stew, followed by prune pie covered in sugar.

'It is the part of France I find most congenial, alive with old legends and fisherfolk laments. There are grottoes and caves, beaches, and forests to wander in. I stayed there when I wrote *Ar More*. One day I shall go back and buy my house.'

His words echoed in her mind as they rode home to Dar al Amra. Duane, in the darkness, had spoken with nostalgia of a far more distant place – a place to which he would not return, for his memories were painful ones.

Sometimes he rode up to Dar al Amra for a nightcap and a sandwich. He would talk with his grandmother out under the old charmed tree that guarded the Court of the Veils, she in her ocelot cape. Now and again he laughed at a tart remark from Nanette, and Isabela, grown restless in the *salon*, would saunter outside ... evidently jealous of the attention he was paying another woman, even though that woman was his grandmother.

Tristan would shoot an amused glance at Roslyn from his seat at the piano, and she would recall that Sunday morning on the headland above Lake Temcina and Duane remarking that he didn't want Isabela to know about their 'little adventure'. Isabela Fernao must have an unnaturally jealous nature if she couldn't bear even Nanette to amuse him!

How could anyone help falling under Nanette's spell? She was so warm-hearted and generous, with a gay sense of humour that had not soured with the years.

Roslyn went to her room each morning to enjoy a chat with her. 'I breakfast in bed because I am lazy,' she said, but there were times when she looked very fatigued, with a hint of blue about her lips, and Roslyn would feel a clutch of anxiety.

'What are you thinking?' Nanette asked one morning. 'That one day your own fair hair must turn white, and your smooth young skin become wrinkled? Does the prospect of old age worry you, my child?'

'Not if I could wear my years as gracefully as you, Nanette.' Roslyn smiled to hide her anxiety at how fragile Nanette was looking this morning. She had picked at her breakfast, now she was lying back against her blue pillows instead of going through her mail, or studying the latest fashions in *Vogue* and *Elle*.

'Grace comes with good memories,' she mused. 'I have many. They are strung like the beads of a rosary and each one gives me joy, sometimes sadness, and very often pleasure. It pleases me to remember how I stood ankle-deep in flowers after my first big stage triumph. A very distinguished young man took me to supper after the show and we had caviar and champagne. At that time, you understand, I had not met Armand. If I had never met him, I think I should have married my distinguished diplomat and become a leading light of Paris society.'

'I don't think you'd have been half as happy as you have been, Nanette,' Roslyn said with conviction. 'You married for love.'

'Yes, my romantic child, I married for love – though I tell you now that I had my misgivings about doing so. Other men seemed more understanding than Armand. They were happy to give in to my whims, to be led rather than followed. Armand gave in to *nobody*. A woman either accepted him as he was, knowing he would cherish her or be cruel as the mood took him, or she turned her back on him and chose a more moderate man for a husband. My family and my friends thought him a barbarian. He was not given to hand-kissing, you see, or paying compliments. He was a man of the soil, rugged as the trees he planted, and unpredictable as the desert winds.

'Each time I saw him I wanted to run away, but,' Nanette gave a nostalgic laugh, 'I ran in circles from him, like a doe from a stag. I had to show some fight, even when the circles narrowed to the circumference of his arms.'

Nanette's eyes dwelt on the girl seated beside her on the canopied bed. Her thin young face was serious, her eyes a lucid grey. 'You have a very untouched look, my child,' the older woman spoke thoughtfully. 'Your heart, I think, has not felt love as I felt it at your age. You would not forget *that*, no matter what other fury you passed through.'

The anchusa-blue eyes were so searching that Roslyn had to avoid them. She looked down at her folded hands, the left atop the right, no longer wearing the engraved ring whose stone blazed as love should. 'Perhaps your Armand was unique,' she tried to speak lightly. 'As strong and compelling as the feelings he awoke in you.'

Nanette put out a hand and tilted Roslyn's chin. She slowly shook her head and smiled. 'No, I have met his match – in all but one respect. My husband was never reserved. He hid nothing from me. This other – he has arrogant reserve. He keeps locked within him the things that hurt him, and this is not a good thing to do. If he were a boy, I might persuade him to confide in me, but he is a man – very much a man – and he guards his secret.'

Nanette sank back against her pillows and her eyes grew shadowed. 'I feel in my bones that it concerns a woman, and I believe he still loves her despite the pain she has caused him.'

The man's name had not been mentioned, but Roslyn knew that Nanette was referring to her half-English grandson.

'Men from boys harbour a lot of romantic illusions about women, but if these are shattered in a painful way, something tender and boyish is killed in the man.' Nanette drew a sigh. 'This has happened to the man to whom I refer – *bah*, now I am being secretive. I speak of my grandson Duane. Did you guess as much, my child?'

Roslyn gave a quick little nod.

'Astute of you, *petite*.' There was an ironical glint in Nanette's eyes. 'Duane has the authority and self-assurance of a bashaw. To most outsiders he reveals little sign of a hurt sensitivity.'

'Mr. Hunter is cynical about women,' Roslyn spoke formally, perhaps because of being called an outsider. 'You are the only person he loves and admires. You are his goddess, Nanette. He has told me so.'

'I am flattered,' Nanette smiled. 'Tell me, do you call him Mr. Hunter to his face?'

Roslyn flushed slightly and thought of some of the things she had called him – to his face.

'He is not a charmer like Tristan, eh? You are never formal with *him*, I have noticed. Does Duane ever join you and Tristan on your desert rides?'

'*No* – I mean, he's always busy about the plantation. Anyway, I'm sure we ride a little too sedately for him.'

'Very likely. He is an Arab in the saddle of that rakish bay of his, and he would spoil outings which you find congenial. He is not easy to know, is he, child? Or to like. A fortress of a man, with no openings left for the assaults of – friendship.'

Roslyn pleated the lace cover of Nanette's bed, then realizing what she was doing she hastily ironed out the pleats with her fingers. 'I do find Tristan good company,' she admitted. 'This afternoon he's taking me to see some historical cave-drawings at a place called Ajina.'

'I am sure you will enjoy your history lesson,' Nanette said dryly. 'Isabela takes a beauty nap while you two are out riding, eh? She is like a golden cat, that one. Lazy and sensuous.'

Yes, Roslyn thought. But she couldn't imagine a man

calling her Miss Puss.

Roslyn and Tristan set out for Ajina at three o'clock that afternoon. It was hot, the lion-coloured sands rolling away in sunshot combers towards the mountains, forcing Roslyn to pull the brim of her hat well down over her eyes to shade them. She wore a long-sleeved blouse to protect her arms from the sun. Across her saddle her cloak lay folded, for when they rode home at dusk-fall the air would have cooled considerably.

They rode along in a companionable silence, and this gave Roslyn a chance to realize that during her chat with Nanette she had not been warned to beware of Tristan's resemblance to Armand ... Nanette no longer seemed to think that she would identify him with his dead brother. He had become a person to her in his own right, congenial, full of knowledge, and always kind.

When they reached the caves, they tethered their mounts to some nearby tamarisks and Tristan produced a torch. They entered the caves, the beam of light stirring the bats that clustered in sleeping groups under the roof. 'They are timid creatures,' Tristan assured her. 'They won't fly at us.'

She hoped not, for they looked furry and rather horrid, like mice with wings. Then she forgot them as she and Tristan examined the chiselled drawings on the walls of rock. There were tusked animals, some of them long-necked and very predatory-looking; hunting scenes and family fire-circles.

'I wonder,' Roslyn murmured, 'if we of today are so very different from those people, squatting in a circle, exchanging gossip and food – and affection.'

'Fundamentals don't change,' Tristan was tracing one of the engraved figures with his finger. 'The human appetites are still very basic. Man must hunt, eat, generate, and die. It is possible, however, that these primitives were happier than we the so-called civilized. They were probably less competitive, for each man could satisfy his aggressions as a hunter and provide his woman with ample furs, steaks and cave-man embraces.'

Roslyn gave a laugh that echoed along the tunnels. 'Do you think women still go for cave-men?'

'You are a woman,' his dark, smiling eyes met hers. 'You tell me.'

'I don't think I'd care to be dragged into a wolf-skinned lair by my hair,' she laughed. 'It's a little too short at the moment, anyway.'

'I hope you are going to let it grow again. You must look like Alice in search of Wonderland with your fair hair on your shoulders.'

'At the moment I am Roslyn in Wonderland.' Her eyes grew serious. 'I've been at Dar al Amra five weeks, and I begin to think that I ought to return to England. Perhaps it would be better – seeing familiar scenes might bring back my memory.'

'You have no people in England, but here you have Nanette, and myself,' Tristan reminded her. 'Think how I would miss you.'

'But I can't go on imposing myself on Nanette's hospitality,' she protested. 'Not indefinitely.'

'Nothing is for ever, *chérie*,' he smiled quizzically. 'You are not unhappy at Dar al Amra, are you? We do our best to make you feel at home.'

'Tristan, it isn't that—'

'I wonder if you really know what it is. Come,' he caught at her wrist, 'we will ride through the village of Ajina on our way home. It is a rather quaint place and I am sure you will be interested in the houses and their inhabitants.'

They made their way out of the caves, untied their horses and remounted. The plain was not quite so hazy with heat, above it the mountains of the Gebel d'Oro licked at the blue sky with forked, tawny tongues. A land to catch at the imagination, to lure and to frighten with its stretches of untamed desert, its gullies gaping like sardonic grins, and its hidden villages such as Ajina, honeycombed with strange Arab dwellings.

Half-naked children ran about, playing in the dust among lumps of masonry. Then they spotted the two riders and at once they came hopping and leaping over the stones to caper about the legs of the horses. They didn't pester for anything, but with enormous dark eyes they gazed up into Roslyn's face and she wished she had some sweets to give them. She said as much to Tristan when the band of urchins had run off down an alleyway.

'These people cling to the old ways,' Tristan told her. 'They don't like strangers to give things to their children.'

'Even a few innocuous sweets?' she exclaimed.

'Look about you, Roslyn. This is a place of ancient taboos, and veiled women who still believe in the power of the Evil Eye.'

The village did have an air of mystery, of women held in awe of superstition, and as her gaze travelled up the rampart of blank doors, one of them abruptly opened to reveal a gaunt, robed figure. Roslyn met dark eyes, glittering above cheekbones almost Mongolian. The man's nose was jutting and hawkish like his beard, and he stared at them as they rode through his village. Roslyn felt uneasy, and was glad when they neared the end of the street, where women were drawing water from a well.

As the women inspected Roslyn from the tips of her riding-boots to her slouch hat, she couldn't help wondering if they despised her boyish clothing, or accepted all things passively. She tried to put herself in the place of one of them, and found her every nerve shrinking from the idea of seclusion in this fortress of a village.

'Will things never change for them?' She turned to gaze back at the black-draped women as she and Tristan rode out of Ajina.

'The headman is old and feudal, but when he dies his son will see to it that changes are made. He wants the children educated, and the adults taught new methods of tilling the land. You would never believe that such harsh land could be made to yield, eh?'

'Hardly,' she said. 'It seems to be very rocky.'

'Ah, but there are underground springs beneath it. I am told the hills, and consequently those houses, must be blasted flat in order to make this crop-growing scheme possible for the villagers.'

'It would make all the difference in their lives, wouldn't it?' Roslyn said eagerly. 'An abundance of crops, maize and wheat – and new houses for those women. Will the scheme be realized, Tristan?'

'I am sure it will. The man who will soon be running the village – you saw him watching us as we rode through – has become a member of a Food Association Board set up by my cousin.'

'By Duane?'

'Yes.' Tristan met her wide-eyed look, and a smile twitched on his lips. 'Duane is greatly interested in these people of the East, far more so than I could ever be. In many ways he is our grandfather all over again, a born colonist, and idealist, suited in every way to the life out here.'

'What if he marries?' she asked.

'If he marries, then the woman will have to fold her tent like Ruth and dwell with him in the desert.'

Roslyn thought of Isabela, who was hardly the type to go 'whither thou goest'. She had a career, a love of cities, and a taking nature rather than a giving one.

'Are you thinking that he might wish to marry Isabela?' Tristan asked.

She nodded.

'Nanette, of course, gave up her career in order to marry my grandfather, and women are unpredictable – yes, I suppose it is possible. *Chérie*,' his voice deepened, 'just look at that sunset!'

Together they gazed in awe as the sun in the west spilled like an oriental vat and splashed the sky and the sands with gold, flame and rose. A brief, savage glory, veiled all too soon by a lilac dusk splintered with stars.

'How beautiful,' Roslyn sighed as she fastened her cloak. 'Yet if it lasted any longer, it would be unbearable.'

Like ghostly riders they made no sound as they rode home across the sands, carrying with them strange impressions of Ajina. When they neared the plantation they heard one of the Arab workers singing plaintively among the trees.

Duane strolled up to dinner that evening, and the air was so balmy and tree-scented that they sat out among the shadows of the Court of the Veils to drink their coffee and talk.

'Roslyn was very interested, Duane, in that crop-growing project you and the future headman of Ajina hope to put into operation.' Tristan bent his head to accept the light Isabela held for his cigar. When he drew back, Roslyn caught the glitter of the singer's eyes fixed on her face. Then the flame snapped out and there was only the faint glow of Isabela's white embroidery dress.

'Unless something is done at Ajina, those people are likely to die out.' The orange eye of Duane's cigar pointed in Roslyn's direction. 'The pot-bellies of the children do strike at the conscience, don't they, Miss Brant?'

'If one has a conscience,' she agreed.

'Did it come as a surprise to learn that I have one?' he drawled.

'Not really.'

'Come now, I hope you aren't pinning wings to my shoulders because I get concerned about a bunch of hungry kids.'

'Wings wouldn't suit you,' she rejoined. 'Mr. Hunter,

may I ask a favour of you?'

'I don't want all this shiny new favour to lose its lustre, so go ahead and ask.'

'Tristan tells me that adults of the village don't like strangers to give sweets to their children. Couldn't you do something to alter that attitude?'

'Why, because you'd like to play Sugar Plum Fairy and hand out candy to the kids?' he asked.

'There's no need to be sarcastic about it,' she said hotly, aware of Isabela's throaty giggle in the dark.'

'The ways of those Saharans might seem strange to you,' he said curtly, 'but even in some parts of the United States there are large communities that cut themselves off from their more progressive neighbours and live as their forebears did. That's okay, if they are able to be self-supporting, but I know, just as you suspect emotionally, that Ajina can't survive as a self-supporting community. But when Europeans start approaching such communities with their modern ideas, patience is the guide word. Archaic notions have to be tolerated until they can be eliminated, no matter how much they try that patience.'

He drew hard on his cigar, making a warning red light in the dark. 'Bear in mind what I've said, Roslyn, and don't go wandering up there alone with a tin of toffees and good intentions the mothers of those kids won't understand. They'll take you for a grey-eyed witch—'

'*Duane*, really! Roslyn is little more than a child herself, a kind-hearted one, who does not fully understand your problems ...' and there, with a sharp catch of her breath, Nanette broke off and caught at the left side of her chest.

'What's the matter, Nanette?' Duane was on his feet in an instant and bending over her.

But for several seconds she couldn't speak, each breath she took seemed to cause her distress. Then the frightening spasm passed and she let Duane lift her into his arms and carry her into the *salon*. Under the lights they saw that her face was pallid and drawn.

'A little brandy will help.' Roslyn hurried to the sideboard where the decanters stood. Behind her, as she opened the cupboard and took out a glass, Duane was saying that a doctor should be sent for. 'Get on the phone to my house, Tristan,' he said. 'Tell my houseboy Da-ud to take the car and fetch Dr. Suleiman up here as fast as possible.'

'Suleiman's an Arab,' Tristan objected.

'What the devil does that matter?' Duane's voice was impatient. 'He's a darned good doctor, and Da-ud will find him quicker than you or me. The nearest French doctor lives in town and he'll take an hour or more getting here.'

'Very well.' Tristan strode off to telephone, and Roslyn sat down beside Nanette and coaxed a few sips of brandy into her. Duane was kneeling beside the divan, his face curiously alien to Roslyn as he spoke in soothing French to his grandmother and stroked her fragile hands.

Isabela stood nearby, wrenching with her fingers at a chiffon handkerchief. Her fingers grew still as Roslyn glanced at Duane and told him not to worry. Her eyes narrowed as she took in the fair head so close in that moment to the coppery, ruffled hair of the man.

Though Duane's face was strange to Roslyn as she looked at him, she felt no stranger to the task of giving comfort to his grandmother. She was in fact reacting instinctively as an air-hostess trained and ready to give aid to a distressed person, and her fingers did not fumble as she removed Nanette's choker of pearls, and placed cushions behind her shoulders so that she was propped up and able to breathe more easily.

There was a calm gentleness about her that combined with the lamplight in her fair hair to give her a look of beauty that made Isabela's eyes gleam catlike as they raked her.

Roslyn wasn't aware of the other girl, only of Nanette .. and Duane.

CHAPTER TWELVE

'A DOCTOR is coming, *ma chère*.' Duane gave his grand-mother a reassuring smile. 'He is a good man and he will soon make you feel better.'

She nodded, and for a long moment her eyes rested upon his face. Then she glanced at Roslyn, who sensed at once that Nanette wished to speak privately to her grandson. She rose and went over to the archway that led out to the Court of the Veils. A night breeze rustled the branches of the big pepper tree, and behind her she heard the low rumble of Duane's voice.

Isabela had not moved her position. It was obvious that she wanted to hear what was being said ... and Roslyn felt certain that Duane was promising to carry on with the work his grandfather had started. The work of the plantation, so far from Lisbon and Paris, and the glitter of the operatic world.

Upon Dr. Suleiman's arrival, Nanette was carried to her room by Duane, who reappeared in the *salon* a few minutes later. Yousef had just brought coffee, and Roslyn poured out while Tristan handed round the sensible-sized French cups.

Isabela had made herself comfortable on a divan, and she beckoned Duane to join her. He did so, sinking down among the cushions with a rather deep sigh.

'Did Dr. Suleiman have anything to say about Nanette?' Tristan asked anxiously.

'You know doctors.' Duane took a gulp of hot coffee. 'They won't commit themselves until they've turned a patient inside out.'

'You are certain this man knows his job?' Tristan persisted.

Duane's gaze flashed upwards. 'I would hardly place Nanette – of all people – in the hands of an incompetent,' he said cuttingly. 'She happens to mean a great deal to me, and for your edification, Dr. Suleiman was trained in Algiers and in England, where he specialized in internal medicine. He could have gone into practice in a city anywhere and earned plenty of money, instead he chose to come and doctor the people of El Kadia. I have called him in several times to attend to accident cases at the plantation and I can assure you his methods are right up to date, and his ability first rate.'

'I was merely asking.' Tristan put out a hand and gripped his cousin's shoulder. 'We are both worried, *mon cher*. It is understandable, for who in the world could take Nanette's place in our hearts?'

Roslyn sipped her coffee, but it didn't infuse much warmth into her body, which had gone curiously cold at Tristan's words. He began to pace about the *salon*, finally he went and sat at the piano, as though only there did he find a measure of peace from his anxious thoughts.

Isabela, her silken legs curled beneath her, was studying Duane's profile under her full eyelids. Roslyn saw the gleam of her eyes as they dwelt on his ruffled hair, then travelled down the lean cheek, past the jutting nose to the compressed lips and hard jaw. What was Isabela thinking – that it was going to be quite a job, enticing such a man to break a promise?

Suddenly, with no sound of footfalls on the tiles of the corridor, a man entered the room. He was slenderly built and though he was wearing a lounge suit, there was no mistaking him for a European. His eyes sloped densely above hollow cheeks, his expression combined shrewdness with a look of age-old patience and humour. His hands were narrow and shapely as a woman's.

'Madame Gerard is now sleeping,' he said in English. 'I assure all of you that there is no cause for alarm – when one is past seventy, the heart grows a little tired. I have prescribed for her from two to three weeks' complete rest in bed, and I would suggest that a nurse be hired. Someone to ensure that Madame remains in her bed.'

'Can you arrange about a nurse, Dr. Suleiman?' Duane asked.

'Of course, Mr. Hunter, if you wish me to.'

'I should have thought it advisable for Madame to be examined by a heart specialist,' Tristan said. 'I am not disputing your word, Dr. Suleiman, but my grandmother did look extremely fatigued, and her breathing was bad.'

'If it will set your mind at rest, *m'sieur*, then by all means call in a specialist.' Dr. Suleiman smiled faintly. 'I repeat, however, that Madame is of an age when the heart is no longer elastic, and there are signs of an anaemia which I should like to examine more fully.'

'Naturally we wish you to keep a check on her, Dr. Suleiman,' Duane said firmly. 'This anaemia would account for the breathlessness, I take it? What about the pain?'

'Heart pain, directly in that region, is not always indicative of disease of the organ, Mr. Hunter. Madame Gerard is strong for her years, I do assure you, but the East will take toll in the end of the soundest of European constitutions, and right now she needs rest and to be treated for anaemia for some time. I am confident that I can remedy this condition for her – if I am permitted to do so.'

'You are, with our thanks, Doctor.' Duane smiled tiredly, and thrust a hand through his shock of copper hair. 'God, what a relief! You can just imagine what we've all been thinking for the past hour.'

The Arab doctor inclined his head, then turned to accept from Roslyn the cup of coffee she had poured out for him. '*J'ai soif, merci,*' he said with a smile.

'I'm English, Doctor.' She smiled back at him. 'If

Madame Gerard is not seriously ill, would it be all right for me to look after her?'

'You are not a nurse, *chérie*,' Tristan exclaimed.

'Air-hostesses have to be able to look after the sick, and Nanette might prefer me to a stranger.' Then she glanced from Tristan to Duane. 'Unless you would prefer someone else, Mr. Hunter?' she added.

'I haven't the sole casting vote on that question,' he said dryly. 'If Tristan wants you, and if Dr. Suleiman finds you suitably qualified, then I am out-voted.'

'The qualifications are fairly simple ones.' Dr. Suleiman was regarding Roslyn with shrewd, interested eyes. 'Madame must be kept in bed, and it will be easier to keep her there if she is attended by someone patient, willing – and charming.'

Roslyn felt herself go pink at the compliment. Duane was watching with cool green eyes as Tristan put an arm around her. 'Miss Brant has amnesia,' he informed the doctor. 'She has been very brave about it.'

'Amnesia is a most interesting condition from a psychological point of view.' The doctor's smile was a mixture of shrewdness and sympathy. 'Mr. Hunter and I were discussing a case of it some time ago. One of his workmen sustained a severe blow on the head and suffered a total loss of memory – but for forty-eight hours only. How long have you had your amnesia, Miss Brant?'

She told him, and he looked thoughtful. 'Amnesia in a sensitive female would be likely to last longer than in a sturdy, extrovert male. It is also possible, Miss Brant, that the past holds something which you don't wish to remember—'

'Don't you know,' Tristan broke in, 'that my brother, Miss Brant's fiancé, was killed in the plane crash in which she received her head injury?'

Dr. Suleiman studied her as he drank his coffee and

then set aside the cup and saucer. 'Yes, your mind could be taking its time to adjust from the shock – very possibly it will take another shock to jolt your memory awake.'

'Not – not another like the crash?' She looked at him aghast.

'By no means.' He shook his head quickly. 'I refer to an emotional shock. In the majority of women the emotions are sensitive as violin strings ... tuned too tightly they will go off key, or they will snap. When this happens, Miss Brant, you will have to face all that you have forgotten. And now,' he consulted his wrist watch, 'I think I will take my leave.'

He turned his attention to Tristan. 'By all means call in a heart specialist to take a look at Madame Gerard, but I think you will find my opinion verified.'

'I'm sure of it, Tristan.' As Duane spoke, Roslyn felt the brief, green flicker of his glance. 'Dr. Suleiman is usually right when he makes a diagnosis.'

He and the doctor then said good night and departed, their voices mingling deeply as they made their way to Duane's car. Roslyn turned to say good night to Isabela, who brushed past her without replying and swept out of the room. Tristan caught Roslyn's eye and shrugged his shoulders.

'Isabela likes to be the *étoile* of all dramas,' he said dryly. 'She did not like it tonight that Duane had his thoughts upon someone other than herself.'

'She's very selfish,' Roslyn said quietly. 'Knowing how much you both love Nanette ...' the words caught in her throat and she began to collect up the coffee cups and to stack them on the tray for Yousef.

Within a matter of days Nanette was feeling much better. She had confidence in Dr. Suleiman and waved away Tristan's suggestion that a specialist be brought in to take a look at her. 'My old heart is bound to feel creaky after seventy-three years of living and loving,' she said. 'The doctor I have knows what he is doing, Tristan.'

All the same she didn't care for the injections that were part of her treatment and after each thrust of the needle she would have a small grumble. 'Soon I shall look like a pincushion,' she said to Dr. Suleiman one morning, as he dabbed antiseptic on her upper arm.

'Come now, you know you are enjoying the way we are all fussing over you,' the doctor smiled. 'My injections are a beauty tonic. Look how they have put the sparkle back into your eyes.'

'Yes, you are a clever rogue of an Arab,' she retorted. 'Why are you working out here in the Sahara when you could be making a fortune elsewhere?'

'Because I am an Arab, madame. A lot needs to be done, and men can't do it if they are sick.'

'Another pioneer,' she groaned. 'Has Duane told you of the funds for a clinic which we wish to put at your disposal?'

He inclined his head.

'Will you accept them?' she asked.

'Will a dog turn its tail on a pound of meat?' he said with dry humour. 'I am profoundly grateful to both of you. I know the gift is made out of understanding and not charity.'

'Duane has too much pride himself to offer anyone charity, Ben Suleiman. I can understand why you two are friends. You have each chosen what you want to do with your lives, and you are both strong enough to put your work before other desires. Such men are always a little frightening – do you not agree, Roslyn?'

Roslyn was tidying up after the doctor. 'It isn't for a nurse to pass judgment on a super being such as a doctor,' she said with a smile.

'Am I alarming, Miss Brant?' he asked.

'Alarming in the sense that you carry life in your hands,' she replied. 'All laymen are in awe of a doctor's knowledge and skill.'

'You cannot be called a layman, Nurse.' He smiled in his grave way. 'You are very able in a sickroom.'

'Thank you, Doctor.' She wore a white overall which he had acquired for her, and she looked quite efficient in it. 'Nanette has been so good to me that I'm very glad I am able to do something for her.'

'*Mon dieu*, how independent the British are!' Nanette raised her hands in Gallic exasperation. 'The child is happy now, you see. She is repaying me for indulging myself by having her with me in this barn of a house.'

'Now don't get excited, Nanette.' Roslyn grinned and plumped her patient's pillows. 'You'll overtire yourself and won't be nice and fresh to receive visitors.'

Even in her sickbed Nanette liked to look at her best, and after Dr. Suleiman had gone, she had Roslyn arrange her hair and lightly make up her face. 'If I look pale and wan I worry those grandsons of mine.' She studied her reflection in the hand-mirror which Roslyn held for her. 'This bedjacket is quite *chic*, no? I was married in a blue silk suit. It was my husband's favourite colour. He used to say that my eyes outshone the desert skies.'

'They are a wonderful colour,' Roslyn assured her.

'Men like women to have nice eyes,' Nanette smiled. 'Yours are huge and fascinating, *ma petite*. Your best feature, incidentally.'

'They're the grey eyes of a witch,' Roslyn said lightly. 'I have to be careful not to cast spells with them.'

A brisk rap on the door followed her words, and in walked the man who had called her a grey-eyed witch.

Though Nanette's room was already bright with flowers, he carried a potted plant that was breaking out into mauve flower, and also something bulky in a carrier bag. He came striding to Nanette's bedside and bent his tall head to kiss her cheek. 'You look very elegant and smell very enticing,' he said fondly.

'Thank you for the plant, Duane, and do sit down. You give me a crick in my neck, you are so tall, *mon brave*.'

He folded his long limbs down into a pastel wicker chair, which creaked alarmingly. 'I feel like a bull in a boudoir.' He shot his rather fierce smile at Roslyn as she took the potted plant from him. 'How is your patient behaving, Nurse? Is she giving you any trouble?'

'None that I can't cope with.' Roslyn put her nose to the mauve flowers, hiding the amusement he induced, so big and clumsy in that chair, in this room with its French furniture. He was far more at home among the barbaric trappings of his own tree-secluded house.

'Each day I can see an improvement in you, Nanette,' he said. 'Ben Suleiman knows his job all right.'

'I like him very much, except when he is jabbing needles in my arm.' His grandmother cocked an eye at the carrier bag Duane was still holding. 'What have you got in there, another present for me?' she asked.

'You are every inch a Frenchwoman,' he teased. 'I could have my laundry in the bag, but right away you assume it is something for you.'

'Of course it is – ah, but then again it could be something for my nurse. A tin of toffees, perhaps?' she added wickedly.

He quirked an eyebrow at Roslyn, then drew out of the carrier the enchanting musical-box that had looked so out of place in his very masculine sitting-room.

He placed it on his grandmother's bed. 'For you, *belle femme*,' he said quietly. 'I thought it might amuse you.'

Nanette touched the figure of the dancing girl, and sudden tears sprang into her eyes. 'But no, Duane, you have always been so fond of *la boîte à musique*. It belonged to Céleste – to your dear mother. I would not dream of taking it from you—'

'I want you to have it, Nanette. You gave it to – *maman*. Still it plays, and the girl still dances. Look, I'll wind it up for you.' He did so and as the music tinkled out, the tiny figure on the lid began to pirouette.

Roslyn was fascinated by the dancing figure, but when she looked at Duane she was struck by the expression in his eyes ... it could only be described as angry pain ... pain he hated to feel. He got to this feet and went over to the latticed window guarding the balcony. A shaft of sunlight fired his hair as he stood there, tall and tough, hardened against pain ... so Roslyn had always thought.

When the tinkling music died away, he swung to face his grandmother. 'It's a woman's toy,' he said. 'I want you to have it.'

'But, *chéri*, I know how much this memento of your dear mother means to you—' then, seeing how set his face was, Nanette added that she would love to have the musical-box and he was a dear to give it to her.

'Come,' she patted the bedside, 'come and talk to me. Tell me about the plantation and how big a harvest we can expect.'

Roslyn left them talking together. She went downstairs, passing the *salon* where Isabela and Tristan were going over the last act of his opera. The music followed her out to the Court of the Veils, haunting and oriental, with slumbering notes of fire in it. She listened as she sat under the pepper-tree.

When Nanette was well again, Roslyn knew that she would pack her bag and leave this desert house for England. Somehow the time had almost come for her to go ...

To run away, cried a small voice inside her. Yes, you'll be running away, and you know it.

She wanted to deny it, but it was true. She would be running away from Dar al Amra because she knew she was emerging out of the mists of her amnesia as a girl who had never loved Armand Gerard. Instinct had told her from the beginning that she had never loved him . . . and when she recovered her memory she wouldn't be able to face Nanette, who trusted her, who had wanted her here because she was a link with her grandson Armand.

Roslyn's gaze wandered round the Court of the Veils . . . here, for the first time in her life, she had been part of a real family, and it would break her heart to leave. To hear no more the workers chanting their Eastern songs in the depths of the plantation. To see no more the sunsets that flared like harlequin opals, and the moon that hung among the stars like a great rose-gold ball. . . .

Suddenly her thoughts had become unbearable and she jumped to her feet and was on the verge of flight when there was a footfall behind her. She swung round and her grey-clouded eyes looked straight up into Duane Hunter's.

Their magnetic green held her, though she wanted more than ever to run away. 'I want to thank you for the very good care you are taking of Nanette,' he said.

'That's all right, Mr. Hunter.' She was backing away from him and couldn't stop. Suddenly she was brought up short against the trunk of a juniper-tree.

'Has something frightened you?' he asked.

She shook her head, framed slim and white-clad by the foliage of the juniper.

'I saw you jump up as though a snake had just slithered across your shoe.' He came a stride closer, towering over her. 'You've done a lot for Nanette in the past two weeks. Perhaps your nerves are a trifle shot?'

'No – I was sitting and thinking, then I suddenly realized that I had to go and see about Nanette's lunch tray.' She moved, but he was blocking her path, so she drew back against the juniper once more.

'You can't wait to dash off indoors, can you?' he mocked. 'Ever since our little adventure at Lake Temcina you get rattled each time I come up here to the house. What are you afraid of? That it's going to come out sooner or later that we spent a night by the lake – in a boat-shed?'

'Don't!' The word broke from her, then because she sounded a trifle desperate, she forced a smile to her lips and gestured at the juniper-tree. 'Never tell a secret by the juniper, Mr. Hunter. It's asking for trouble.'

'Really?' His mouth quirked into a smile, and suddenly his desert-brown hands were against the trunk of the tree, one either side of her fair head, and she was his captive as she had been down on the shore at Lake Temcina.

'You walk into trouble too easily, Miss Brant,' he drawled.

'It certainly looks like it,' she agreed, but without the spirit she usually brought to a sparring match with him. The air this morning was sultry, leaden, and that was how she felt. Too passive to resist, even if those mocking lips had come hunting for a fight.

'What's up?' Suddenly his green eyes narrowed. 'Have you been eating any desert fruit without first giving it a good wash?'

She smiled faintly. Trust Duane to think it was her tummy that ached!

'The air this morning is rather close,' she said. 'Talking about fruit, you might pluck me a couple of oranges so I can give your grandmother some juice with her lunch.'

He turned away at once, plucked the required oranges and tossed them to her. 'We may be in for a sandstorm,' he said. 'The air is always a bit mucky when one is due.'

'When will it come?' she asked anxiously. 'They're rather terrible, aren't they?'

'When a sandstorm is at its height, nothing can be seen for yards,' he told her. 'The desert afterwards can be quite featureless – but you'll be perfectly safe here at Dar al Amra, and the storm shouldn't break for hours yet.'

'I hope it won't upset Nanette,' she said, looking troubled.

'I'll come back later,' he had reached the slave door and was opening it, 'and we'll all do our bit to keep her mind off the storm. By the way, I shouldn't go out if I were you.'

'No,' she said absently, and watched him duck through the slave door. It clanged shut behind him, leaving a silence that was strangely acute, until Roslyn realized that the music from the *salon* had ceased. She turned to go indoors ... where under the archway facing the *salon* she came face to face with Isabela.

'How busy you are these days, Roslyn.' The singer was standing with her back to one of the columns, her hands at either side of her slowly clenched and unclenched against the marble. 'I see you have been plucking oranges for your patient.'

'Yes.' Roslyn could feel her heart beating nervously as she faced the other girl. If Isabela had been standing here for some time, then she would surely have heard all that Duane had said in that carrying voice of his!

'I am useless at nursing people,' Isabela's voice was mellow as honey. 'But I have been wondering what small thing I could do to be of use – you look so worn out, poor dear. I know! I could take you for a drive this afternoon. Some air would do you good.'

Roslyn gazed at the singer in sheer amazement. She had expected anything but an overture of friendship. 'It's kind of you to suggest a drive, Isabela,' she said, 'but Nanette gets restless if I leave her too long.'

'You take your duties too seriously,' Isabela said with a shrug. 'Very well, if you don't want to come for a drive with me, then we will say no more about it. Tristan, by the way, expects to be working most of the day. He has hit a musical snag which will evidently take some hours to unravel.'

Roslyn had been looking forward to a gallop that afternoon, despite the coming storm, and now on impulse she said she wouldn't mind going out for a short drive. 'I have a slight headache,' she admitted.

Isabela's dark brows lifted. 'Perhaps the injury to your head is troubling you, eh?'

'Perhaps.' Roslyn forced a smile to her lips. 'A half hour's spin through the desert might blow away the cobwebs, but we mustn't be out too long because—'

'Because of Nanette, I know.' The next moment Isabela was hurrying away, calling over her shoulder. 'I am looking forward to our drive – so very much.'

She was gone and Roslyn was alone in the corridor . . . remembering the danger-green of Duane's eyes when he had warned her not to go out that afternoon. But she felt so restless, and the air was so sultry that it was even an effort to walk as far as the kitchen. 'Yousef,' she said at once, 'when will the storm come?'

He stood very still, as if listening to the far-off shuffling of the sand. 'Not yet,' he said. 'Maybe this evening.'

CHAPTER THIRTEEN

SERVANTS were going round the house securing doors and window shutters by the time Roslyn ran downstairs to join Isabela. She had not told Nanette that they were going for a drive. With the sandstorm coming on, Nanette would worry about them and not get her proper amount of rest.

Isabela was already seated in the car, wearing a shantung suit and a brimmed hat with spotted chiffon tied round the high crown. She opened the passenger door for Roslyn, who slid in beside her, clad in a youthful blue cotton dress, her eyes shaded also by a brimmed hat.

'How sultry the air has become.' Isabela started up the car and they drove out under the high Moorish arch on to the cool green track that ran through the plantation and joined the desert highway. As they passed Duane's secluded house, Isabela glanced back as though searching the veranda for a tall, drill-clad figure. But the only figure that Roslyn glimpsed was a boyish one in a white *gandourah*. Da-ud the houseboy, no doubt.

'I really don't know how Duane can bear to live among all those trees,' Isabela remarked. 'At night they must be alive with the noise of cicadas and frogs.'

'I expect he's used to trees,' Roslyn said. 'Think of all the years he spent in Amazonian forests.'

'Living in the wilds is just a habit he has got into.' Isabela blared the horn as one of the plantation workers crossed the track along which they were driving. 'Habits can be broken. Also a man with his drive could make far more money directing a business from a desk rather than spending his life as a planter.'

'Perhaps he's one of those people who get satisfaction

out of being among things that grow. I can't imagine Mr. Hunter behind a desk,' Roslyn spoke firmly. 'I should think such a life would stifle him.'

Isabela made no reply to that until they were out on the highway and the needle of the speedometer had moved forward into the seventies. The car sped along past the sandy wastes where chalk-green scrub and thorn bushes made dabs of colour. The sky was a hot blue and could not be looked at with the naked eye.

'Why do you refer to Duane in such a formal manner?' Isabela drawled. 'I am sure there has not always been such formality between you.'

'Indeed there has,' Roslyn said at once. 'Somehow we have never hit it off as friends.'

'How did you hit it off as lovers?'

For a moment Roslyn couldn't believe that she had heard correctly. Her glance flew to Isabela, whose profile was carved ivory beneath the brim of her hat, encircled by the streaming chiffon.

'You heard me,' Isabela snapped. 'Just as I heard Duane out on the patio this morning. You were afraid, he said, of it coming to light that you and he had spent a night together at Lake Temcina. Why afraid? Because Tristan thinks you a little innocent, and Nanette believes you loved her darling Armand?'

'Stop it!' Roslyn ordered. 'None of it's true, what you're thinking. Duane and I were trapped down on the lake-shore by a landslide. We had to stay in a boat-shed until the morning, but I can assure you that he did not make love to me.'

'Why were you down on the shore together?' Isabela's hands were gripping the wheel of the car, which was hurtling along over the round-headed stones of the road.

'We were not together — not right away.' Roslyn had to raise her voice above the rush of the wind, one hand holding on to her hat to keep it from flying off her head. 'I felt like a walk, and he must have had the same idea as me, that the lake looked mysterious and inviting in the moonlight. But I no more wanted to run into him than he wanted to have the responsibility of me for the night. The path back to the hotel was all but swept away – we couldn't do anything else but wait for daylight to come.'

'Why did you keep your little adventure such a big secret?'

It was a pertinent question, but Roslyn was in no mood for the sparing of feelings ... hers were not being spared by this inquisition.

'Duane wanted it that way,' she said. 'It was his idea that we say nothing. I think he must have known that you would jump to the wrong conclusion.'

'Or that I would jump to the right one,' Isabela said sharply. 'Most cats look alike in the dark – and I presume the boat-shed was pretty dark – and they all purr when they are stroked.'

'Some scratch, Miss Fernao.' Roslyn's eyes were blazing. 'I think it's insulting of you to suppose that Duane would make love to any girl he happened to be alone with for a few hours – or that I would let him! I'm sure he finds the majority of women quite resistible – even the beautiful ones.'

She hit a nerve that time. Isabela shot her a glare that headed them straight into a pothole, causing a bump that rattled Roslyn's teeth. 'You've got what we came driving for,' she said tartly, 'now let's go home. Besides, that sky is beginning to look a bit peculiar.'

A saffron glare was creeping in behind the blue, and the heat was pressing down on the open-top car now Isabela had slowed down their speed.

'Perhaps you will be obliged to share this storm with me,' Isabela drawled.

'I don't think either of us would enjoy that – do you?'

Roslyn was tensed up, to the pitch where she wanted to grab at the wheel and turn the car herself, back towards the direction of Dar al Amra. All around the desert stretched away in an aridity broken only by the distant Gebel d'Oro, which seemed to blend today with a fire-coloured sky.

'What did you talk about — that night?' pursued her inquisitor.

'His father, their place in Kent where Mr. Hunter now lives.'

'If you got caught in the downpour, you must both have been very wet.'

'We were.' Exasperation had got the better of Roslyn. 'We had to strip and dry off. Tell me, Isabela, are we driving back to the scene of the crime?'

Roslyn had a sense of humour, but she didn't reckon on her companion's lack of one. The road ahead was bare of traffic, and as Isabela turned the car, the chiffon on her hat blew in her eyes. She pushed at it with her hand, and the next moment the filmy scarf was sailing through the air, to land on the dusty road some yards behind the car. Isabela braked and they halted. 'Do you mind getting the scarf for me?' she asked Roslyn. 'I am sentimentally attached to it.'

Roslyn opened the door beside her and stepped out on to the road. She ran obligingly back to where the length of chiffon lay curled like a spotted snake. As she picked it up, she heard the car start up. She whirled round ... hardly able to believe her eyes as the car shot away and she was left running after it, in its dust trail.

'Isabela,' she cried out, *'wait for me!'*

She was sure that the car would stop before it went over a rise on the road ahead. But it didn't. It dropped out of sight, and when Roslyn reached and mounted the rise, all out of breath, the car was being swallowed up by distance and dust.

It was unbelievable that Isabela had done such a thing, left her on this desert road to walk all those miles back to Dar al Amra. A wedge of anger mixed with tears filled her throat. What a simpleton she had been to trust Isabela ... hadn't she been warned by Tristan that people of Isabela's temperament could be savagely jealous?

Oh, but surely she would return and pick her up. Even Isabela wouldn't be mean enough to leave her stranded like this, miles from home ... with a sandstorm coming on.

Roslyn pulled her lips into control and trudged on, hoping any minute to see the open-top car heading back towards her. The chiffon scarf trailed along in her hand. Soon her cotton dress was sticking to her, and her bare sandalled feet were hot from the stones of the road. She decided that it would be easier to walk on the sand, which crunched underfoot like burnt toast.

She tried to work out how long it would take her to reach the plantation on foot. She and that vixen of a woman had been out in the car about three-quarters of an hour, which meant that right now she was a long way from home. It would surely be nightfall before she reached the house, and from the look of that sky she would be at the mercy of the sandstorm before long.

A dark vapour was drifting across the sun, which was like an inverted cauldron of molten gold. Thick gold that didn't pour down, but which was distilled in an oppressive, slow sliding of warmth. Roslyn was grateful for this, at least. It was better to be slowly broiled than crisped.

What, she wondered, would they say at Dar al Amra when Isabela returned without her?

Nothing, she reminded herself. She had not told Nanette where she was going, and Tristan had shut himself in his room with his lunch and his guitar to work on an obstinate passage of music. She had not seen him all the morning. And she wished to goodness she had not

176

seen Duane. That conversation with him on the patio was the cause of her present predicament.

Her heart twisted oddly, and she stood still as she thought she heard something. Yes, a distinct shuffling sound . . . the sound of leagues of sand shifting in the wind that would rise suddenly, like an angry giant. She gave a shiver, and then her heart was in her throat and she was running on to the road as a vehicle came steadily towards her in a cloud of dust.

It was a Renault wagon . . . conjured like Cinderella's coach out of space and the growing fear that Roslyn had been feeling increasingly.

'Hey!' she yelled, waving her arm. 'Please . . . can you give me a lift!'

The wagon braked in a haze of dust, and Roslyn ran gratefully to the side of it . . .

'What the devil,' said the driver, 'are you doing all alone out here?'

Roslyn blinked her sweat-tangled lashes, and the brown, green-eyed face came into clearer focus. 'Oh,' she said, 'it's you.'

'Yes,' he mocked, 'me.' He leaned forward and opened the door with which she was fumbling. She climbed in beside him, wearily wondering what she had ever done to put Fate so against her. It would have to be Duane who rolled up to witness her latest misadventure.

'Well,' he said, arms crossed on the wheel, 'I'm waiting for an explanation, miss.'

'Your girl-friend,' she said shakily, 'dumped me here in the middle of nowhere.'

'My *who*?' He was looking at her as though at a nitwit.

'I was a nitwit all right, when I agreed to come out driving with Isabela.' Roslyn now had more control over her voice, but less over her temper. 'She must be neurotic, imagining that we – you and I spent the night together at Lake Temcina for the fun of the thing.'

'So that's it,' he drawled, leaning back to light himself a cheroot. His nostrils thinned and ejected tangy smoke. 'Isabela heard us talking together this morning, eh?'

Roslyn nodded. Her throat was so dry that it hurt to speak.

'What's the matter?' Brown fingers tipped the brim of her hat and touched her moist temple. 'Child, how long have you been out under that sun?'

'About half an hour,' she said huskily. 'I'm so dry—'

At once he reached over to the back seat of the wagon and there was a delicious gurgling sound as he handed her a leather water-bottle. She unscrewed the top and gulped down about half a pint of the cool, longed-for water. Some of it ran down her chin and fell in cool drops on her throat.

'I was dying for a drink.' She smiled gratefully as she handed back the container. 'Thank you.'

He made sure the top was well screwed on, then he tossed the container behind him. He then opened the map compartment in front of him and took out of it a fistful of small yellow limes. These he dropped into her lap. 'Water quenches a thirst, but the fire still smoulders,' he grinned. 'Suck those limes. The best remedy I know for easing a touch of desert throat.'

She tucked into a lime right away, and found it juicy and tart. 'Delicious,' she sighed. 'Manna from heaven.'

He smiled through his cheroot smoke, as though at a child. The engine of the Renault throbbed away, but it didn't quite drown the weird shuffling sound creeping across the desert.

'There's going to be quite a storm,' Duane said quietly. 'Did Isabela know?'

Roslyn licked a globule of juice from her lip. 'I don't suppose she thought of that. Her scarf – this one – blew out of the car and she asked me to get it for her. I – I didn't dream she would drive off and leave me stranded.'

'She's like most neurotics.' Duane flicked ash out of the open window beside him. 'Fascinating charmers, with less sense of wrongdoing than children. I knew what Isabela was like from the moment I met her. Gorgeous to look at, totally absorbed in herself, unscrupulous to the tips of her fingers. Such people just don't care about hurting others. Their own desires are all that count.'

He drew hard on his cheroot, and when Roslyn glanced at him she saw that he was gazing straight ahead of him, his face a brown, stony, chiselled mask. He was looking a hard fact in the face, and Roslyn knew that it was hurting him.

'My own mother was like Isabela,' he said quietly. 'So lovely to look at . . . so utterly selfish to know.'

What he had said was so unexpected that Roslyn didn't take in its significance for several moments. Then as they moved forward, her stunned thoughts moved and the crashing truth hit her.

The woman who had hurt Duane so badly had been his *mother*. Céleste, the adored daughter of Nanette . . . the woman he couldn't talk about because he couldn't bear to hurt his grandmother.

'My mother ran out on my dad when I was a boy,' he went on. 'She got bored with my father, fed up with our jungle home. She ran away with a wealthy Brazilian who owned a large coffee *fazenda*. They dived off to Lima – where only a few days later they were both killed in an earthquake. Dad never really got over the shock. He always believed that if he had gone after her, he might have persuaded her to return home with him. I doubt it. I was just a kid and though I loved her because she was my mother, I had witnessed the rows, the reconciliations and the torment which she caused my father.

'There had been other men beside the Brazilian,' Duane added harshly. 'Affairs which my dad forgave because he knew he had been wrong to marry Céleste Gerard. He was

179

on the point of throwing in his job for her sake, when this Brazilian fellow came along. I remember him, though I've forgotten all the others. He was her sort. The type she should have married ... not a planter. Not a man who needed – well, a different sort of life ... a life close to nature.'

He fell quiet, and Roslyn listened to the drumming of her heart and the rising of the wind as the landscape darkened all around. The atmosphere was one of melancholy, and Roslyn felt sand on her lips, and grains of it were clinging to her moist forehead.

'I'm so sorry, Duane,' she said. What else could she say, that it was awful to lose a mother twice over, to see her run away, and then hear that death had claimed her?

'I don't want to frighten you,' he was having to raise his voice above the growing roar of the wind and the lash of sand against the windshield, 'but it looks as though we're running into the storm head-on.'

'I'm not frightened – not now,' she said, and oddly enough it was true, even though the wind was howling like so many cats chained together. She felt Duane's glance and met his grimly humorous smile. She smiled back, for now she understood what had made this man so seemingly hard and unfeeling.

'It seems as though we're doomed to share storms together,' he said.

'I should have hated to be alone in this,' she gave a shiver. 'Thank heaven you came along when you did.'

'I had some business to see to at Ajina—' there he broke off as a great gust of sand blew right over the wagon and blinded the front windows. Again, and then again this happened, so that they seemed to be driving through an impenetrable fog. Every second the wind was growing more forceful, they were right in the midst of the storm when suddenly a giant hand seemed to lift the wagon and throw it bodily to one side of the road. Duane fought with the wheel as Roslyn was pitched forward against the controls.

A cry of pain broke from her as her forehead came in contact with something hard ... she felt nauseated, and then slid stunned into a small heap as Duane braked furiously and the wagon bucked to a halt in the raging sandstorm.

She felt an arm around her, and water was being gently dabbed against her throbbing forehead. Her eyes blinked open and met the keen anxiety of Duane's.

'W-where are we?' she asked, dazed. 'Did we crash?'

He shook his head and held his water flask so she could take a drink. 'There,' he murmured, 'are you feeling a little better?'

'She nodded, and gazed in wonderment at the shattering gentleness of the face that had always looked anything but gentle. 'I – I feel as though I've got a bump,' she said unsteadily.

'You have, my dear,' then she heard him swallow harshly. 'It's a lucky thing you hit your forehead and not your eye.'

'Mmm,' her head moved drowsily against his shoulder. 'What's that roaring noise? Is it – in my head?'

'It's all right,' he held her close in his arms as the blinding waves of sand crashed over their shelter. 'Sandstorms make a fearful racket, but we're quite safe, shut in here together.'

The roaring grew louder, and with a sudden little sob of fear she buried her face in his shoulder and clutched at him as the world spun round and she thought she was going to pass out again. Her fingernails dug into him, though she wasn't aware of the fact. All she knew was that Duane was the only solid object in her spinning world and she held on to him, shuddering as the darkness was split open and the truth rushed in, causing her the same pain that the eyes feel when a light is suddenly switched on in a dark room.

After a moment or two she felt a hand soothing her brow. 'Duane?' she whispered.

'Yes, my dear,' his hand stroked gently and the pain was going, 'what is it you want to tell me?'

'Duane,' his name broke from her, 'I'm not Roslyn Brant. *I never was.*'

'You're Juliet, of course,' he said. 'Juliet Grey.'

'Yes,' she breathed. 'Everyone thought I was Roslyn because of the ring, and looking a little like her.'

'Can you remember the crash?' Duane asked – in that voice that was so shatteringly gentle.

'It was awful,' her fingers clenched his shoulder. 'I was standing in the aisle of the plane talking to Roslyn and Armand ... suddenly everything went dark, the whole plane shuddered, and the last thing I was conscious of was clutching the hand which Roslyn threw out towards me. Her engagement ring was on that hand. I must have pulled it off as the crash tore us apart.'

'Yes, that's what must have happened.' Duane put a hand beneath her chin and tilted her face so that he could study her features in the dimness of their shelter. 'You and the real Roslyn only resembled each other on the outside, I think.'

'She was much more carefree, but because we were the same build and we both had fair hair which we wore shoulder-length when not in uniform, most of the pilots used to mistake us for sisters. She and Armand were very much in love. It always mystified me that love could be forgotten as easily as I seemed to forget it – and the answer is such a simple one. My heart belonged to no one when the plane crashed. I was just a stewardess on the journey, not Roslyn Brant on her way with her fiancé to meet his family.'

She looked at Duane with the open eyes of Juliet. 'What made you think that I might not be the real Roslyn?' she asked.

'Better than most, Juliet, I know that men do fall for girls unsuited to them,' he said. 'I wondered whether Armand had done so. Whether that gay young cousin of mine had fallen under the spell of a quiet girl, a deep girl who looked as though the woods were her natural home. But just prior to his engagement I had a letter from Armand in which he rhapsodized – as Frenchmen will – about his girl. So chic she might almost be French herself. So very gay-natured, with a love of dancing which equalled his own.'

'So that was why you made me dance with you – that evening – that Lake Temcina evening.' She half-smiled, and her eyes lifted from his throat to his chin, to his mouth. A quiet girl, he had said. A deep girl. He had made those qualities sound wonderful, as though he admired them beyond gaiety and beauty.

'I never cared much for dancing,' she said. 'Roslyn and I were always friends, but the only thing we really had in common was the orphanage. We were both heartily glad to get away from that place.'

'I can imagine,' Duane said gruffly.

'Institutions are always cold, you see, and charity isn't the same as love.' She drew a sigh. 'You have to invent a family for yourself, or find one in the pages of books. You have to imagine the kisses you never had as a child, and if I had been more like Roslyn I should have taken the kisses of some of the pilots we flew with and got over my loneliness. But we only looked alike, we never thought alike, or really wanted the same things.

'On the plane, just before the crash, I was saying how lucky I thought she was because soon she would be part of Armand's family. Subconsciously, perhaps, that was why I put myself in her shoes after the crash – but it wasn't her fiancé I wanted, it was his family.'

'You can still be part of his family,' Duane reminded her.

'No,' she shook her head. 'I shall be going back to England.'

'Don't you care enough for Tristan?' he demanded.

'I care for him very much – as a friend,' she replied. 'And that is how he cares for me.'

Duane's eyes were tigerish in the gloom as they raked her face. 'Are you sure of that?' He spoke savagely. 'You said that at the time of the crash your heart belonged to no one – what about now?'

'My heart is my own business. Suddenly she was struggling with him, for all at once it hurt too much to want to be close to him. 'Duane, let me go!'

'Not just yet!' His savagery seemed to be getting out of control. 'You've said often enough that you don't want my touch, or my friendship, so I've nothing to lose if I do *this*.'

'This' was being tipped over his arm ... being lost for an eternity of breathless, unimaginable seconds in his kiss. His mouth on hers was relentless, hurting her until she ceased to struggle ... then, eyes closed, senses fully awake, she surrendered to the kiss that searched through all her being until it plundered the heart right out of her.

'Now you can slap my face,' he said at last against her mouth.

'Why?' she whispered, still dizzy and shaken by his kiss and the complete awakening which it had brought.

'I thought you might want to – after that,' he said huskily.

'I feel much too weak,' she sighed. 'Duane, you strange man.'

'Sure, a rugged fool who's best at handling trees,' he agreed wryly. 'Someone who once thought that love was just another name for getting hurt.'

'Love?' She spoke tentatively. 'Am I a little storm-crazy, or do you mean what you are saying?'

'I mean what I am saying, and feeling.' His arms tightened round her. 'It's your feelings I'm worried about, Juliet.'

'Juliet,' she murmured after him. 'I feel brand-new, as though life is only just beginning for me – Duane, why were you cruel to me at times?'

'Because I didn't dare to be kind,' he said gruffly. 'I couldn't believe that rare, kind simplicity still existed. Like a jungle boor I had to keep on testing you – no wonder there have been times, Juliet, when you've wanted to slap my face.'

She smiled and drew a finger down the hard cleft in his cheek, savouring this moment of heartfelt joy and clarity of mind. This ravishment in feeling his muscular shoulder under her cheek, the warmth without, and the love within.

'You will have to teach me to be humble, and human, my dear,' he said.

'Darling tyrant,' she laughed against his throat, 'I don't want you humble, and you feel very human to me right now.'

'But I want to make up for hurting you,' his lips brushed warm across the bump on her forehead. 'How do I do that?'

'By never doubting me,' she said gently. 'I love you, Duane. I want to be near you, all my life. I want to care for you, and love away the bitterness you learned as a boy. We've both been lonely—'

'Too lonely, *ma mie*.' His arms crushed her to him. 'But I must work in the forest and the desert – could you share them with me?'

'Easily,' she smiled. 'I have a Ruth-like nature. Whither thou goest, Duane, I'll follow and be happy.'

He kissed her, gently then fiercely. Outside their shelter the tempest was breaking, the wind was dying down, the sands were settling into stillness. Juliet rested against Duane's shoulder, home, found, safe in the strength of the man she had fought and finally come heart to heart with. She loved and was loved, and the knowledge was sweet.

'Poor Roslyn,' she murmured. 'But they are together, she and her love. For always.'

When the storm had died quite away, she and Duane drove home to Dar al Amra. There was much to explain to his family, but first they stopped at Duane's house among the trees and he led her inside. There he took from a little box the ring which Nanette had given him for his bride-to-be. He slipped it on to the third finger of Juliet's left hand, a golden ring set with a pearl and a diamond. A lovers' ring. The pearl symbolic of the woman, the diamond of the man.

A Romeo and Juliet ring.

BARBARA DELINSKY
Fingerprints

Carly Quinn is a
woman with a past.
Born Robyn Hart, she
was forced to don a new
identity when her intensive
investigation of an arson-ring
resulted in a photographer's death
and threats against her life.

Ryan Cornell's entrance into her life
was a gradual one. The handsome
lawyer's interest was piqued, and then
captivated, by the mysterious Carly—a
woman of soaring passions and a
secret past.

Available in October wherever paperbacks books are sold,
or send your name, address and zip or postal code, along with
a check or money order for $4.25 (includes 75¢ postage and
handling) payable to Harlequin Reader Service, to:
Harlequin Reader Service
In the U.S.: P.O. Box 52040, Phoenix, AZ 85072-2040
In Canada: P.O. Box 2800, Postal Station "A", 5170 Yonge Street,
Willowdale, Ont. M2N 5T5

FP-1

RIDE A PAINTED PONY

by **BEVERLY SOMMERS**
The third
HARLEQUIN AMERICAN ROMANCE
PREMIER EDITION

A prestigious New York City publishing company decides to launch a new historical romance line, led by a woman who must first define what love means.

Harlequin
JANET DAILEY
Collector's Edition 2

Volumes #7 through #12

Once again, Harlequin is pleased to present a specially designed collection of 12 exciting love stories by one of the world's leading romance authors. Each edition contains two of Janet Dailey's most requested titles.

Available now wherever paperback books are sold, or available through Harlequin Reader Service. Simply complete and mail the coupon below.

Harlequin Reader Service

In the U.S.
P.O. Box 52040
Phoenix, AZ 85072-2040

In Canada
5170 Yonge Street, P.O. Box 2800,
Postal Station Q, Willowdale, Ont. M2N 5T5

Please send me the following editions of the Harlequin Janet Dailey Collector's Edition 2. I am enclosing my check or money order for $2.95 for each copy ordered, plus 75¢ to cover postage and handling.

☐ 7   ☐ 8   ☐ 9   ☐ 10   ☐ 11   ☐ 12

Number of books checked _____ @ $2.95 each =	$	_____
N.Y. state and Ariz. residents add appropriate sales tax	$	_____
Postage and handling	$	.75
I enclose _____	TOTAL $	_____

Please send check or money order. We cannot be responsible for cash sent through the mail.) Price subject to change without notice.

NAME _____
                       (Please Print)

ADDRESS _____ APT. NO. _____

CITY _____

STATE/PROV. _____ ZIP/POSTAL CODE _____

ID-N

Harlequin reaches
into the hearts and minds
of women across America
to bring you

Harlequin American Romance™

Enter a uniquely exciting new world with

Harlequin American Romance T.M.

Harlequin American Romances are the first romances to explore today's love relationships. These compelling novels reach into the hearts and minds of women across America... probing the most intimate moments of romance, love and desire.

You'll follow romantic heroines and irresistible men as they boldly face confusing choices. Career first, love later? Love without marriage? Long-distance relationships? All the experiences that make love real are captured in the tender, loving pages of **Harlequin American Romances.**

What makes American women so different when it comes to love? Find out with **Harlequin American Romance!**

Send for your introductory FREE book now!

Get this book FREE!

Mail to:

Harlequin Reader Service

In the U.S.	In Canada
2504 West Southern Ave.	P.O. Box 2800, Postal Station A
Tempe, AZ 85282	5170 Yonge St., Willowdale, Ont. M2N 5T5

YES! I want to be one of the first to discover **Harlequin American Romance.** Send me FREE and without obligation *Twice in a Lifetime.* If you do not hear from me after I have examined my FREE book, please send me the 4 new **Harlequin American Romances** each month as soon as they come off the presses. I understand that I will be billed only $2.25 for each book (total $9.00). There are no shipping or handling charges. There is no minimum number of books that I have to purchase. In fact, I may cancel this arrangement at any time. *Twice in a Lifetime* is mine to keep as a FREE gift, even if I do not buy any additional books. 154 BPA NAXG

Name _____ (please print)

Address _____ Apt. no. _____

City _____ State/Prov. _____ Zip/Postal Code _____

Signature (If under 18, parent or guardian must sign.)

AMR-SUB-3